# TALC

## A Haitian Zombie Story

### Jenna Chrisphonte

AyiboBooks

New York  Bruxelles

PUBLISHED BY AYIBOBOOKS
A division of CHRISPHONTE LLC
New York      Bruxelles
chrisphonte.com

AyiboBooks is a trademark of Chrisphonte LLC.

Baron Samedi sequined vèvè art by Valentin Valris

Library of Congress Control Number: 2019936876

Chrisphonte, Jenna
Talc: A Haitian Zombie Story/ Jenna Chrisphonte.- 1st ed.

ISBN 978-1-7337563-0-3

*For my mother, Guerda Phipps Chrisphonte, whose silent suffering made my fight possible.*

# CONTENTS

I am induced to thank my Creator for having, from early life, bestowed upon me the blessing of poverty. Sir, it is a blessing – for if there be any human sensation more ethereal and divine than all others, it is that which feelingly sympathizes with misfortune.

Thaddeus Stevens

# 1 TI JOCELYNE

*Okap, Haiti*

The morning dew subsided as Okap prepared for carnival. Distant drum beats forced Ti Jocelyne from the sponge mattress on the floor. She needed to get to market and prepare for dinner before the crowds made it an impossible to walk through town. Her mental list was on repeat: pork shoulder without the worms, dried *djondjon* mushrooms and sweet peas. When Ti Jocelyne returned, her daughter, Jessica, was playing in the alleyway in front of their hovel. The neighborhood children commandeered the tobacco vendor's baby goat and were ecstatic to race their newly acquired kid.

In the rear courtyard, Ti Jocelyne scooped six small bowls of water from a large plastic drum. She lit a rickety triangle coal fire to nestle a dented aluminum pot. A fragrant layer of chopped onions, scotch bonnet pepper, sprigs of fresh thyme, sweet peas and mounds of pounded garlic filled the air. She added bowls of water until the pot came to a full boil. Ti Jocelyne cut a piece of old pantyhose, stuffed a handful of dried *djondjon* mushrooms into the material, tied knots on both ends and threw it into the pot. The water turned a mysterious black hue while green sweet peas bobbled to the surface. She poured three measured bowlfuls of washed white rice into the dark mixture before giving it another stir.

The pork was unwrapped and meticulously cut into pieces with even ratios of skin, fat and meat. The chunks in the red plastic bowl were drizzled in lime juice, vinegar and salt to clean the meat. A quick toss to discard the acidic water onto the concrete courtyard was necessary before adding a fresh serving of lime, vinegar, salt, pepper, ground garlic, scallion paste, a crushed Maggi cube and a sliced yellow scotch bonnet pepper. Meanwhile, the boiling *djondjon* rice water evaporated into deeper shades of black. She stirred the rice carefully so it wouldn't stick to the bottom of the pot but avoided turning it into a sticky pasty mess with impatient stirring. To simmer the rice, she muffled the fire's intensity by sprinkling a handful of soil over the edges of the coal fire. Ti Jocelyne removed the *djondjon* knot and simmered the rice with a scratched metal cover. Ti Jocelyne stuck two fingers into the pork shoulder chunks to check the seasoning and acidity levels; she placed another small pot on an adjacent open triangle coal fire to stew the pork chunks until they were ready to be dropped in blazing oil. A buried cough escaped from the next room.

Didoune's years made it harder to move and she was resting in bed before the inescapable noise of carnival came. They ate dinner at two o'clock but she taught Ti Jocelyne to cook first thing in the morning before the day imposed itself. Didoune limped to the back of the room, poured water into a chipped white enamel bowl and dunked a torn pink towel. She wiped underneath her arms, behind her ears, underneath her breasts and eventually wiped the lips of her vagina and between her butt cheeks. Her skin had become soft with the years and could be pulled away from the bones in ways unimaginable in her youth. She reached for her bottle of talcum powder and squeezed a puff underneath her arms and across her chest until overwhelmed by the fresh cool scent.

Didoune went into the backyard and Ti Jocelyne was frying the pork chunks into *griot*. The drums were getting closer. Jessica ran into the back courtyard and threw her talc covered arms around Ti Jocelyne's hips. The little girl shared her mother's petite frame but not her complexion. Jessica's butterscotch skin,

3

caramel curls and hazel eyes contrasted against her mother's smooth coffee complexion, black cotton hair and obsidian eyes. The little girl was covered in talcum powder and left tiny handprints on her mother's calves and ankles before quickly running back into the street. Ti Jocelyne was surprised. Those type of carnival antics didn't occur until the early evening hours. She extinguished the coal fire and used a perforated plastic dome to keep the flies off the food.

Ti Jocelyne walked through the narrow living space connecting the two rooms to the front alleyway. It was carnival and Ti Jocelyne braced herself for the unexpected. People wore ridiculous outfits with crazy hairstyles; some dressed their goats while others paraded painted roosters. Sooner than Ti Jocelyne stepped outside, Jessica ran back to her mother. White talcum powder hid her face, arms, hair and yellow dress. The little girl cried while holding onto her mother.

"Little one, what's taken a hold of you?"

"Zombies, they're outside everywhere."

"Don't occupy yourself with people who are talking about stupid things."

"But I saw them; I saw them with my own two eyes."

Ti Jocelyne remained incredulous while Didoune grabbed a clean towel to wipe the powder out of Jessica's eyes. Ti Jocelyne stepped into the front entranceway and was greeted by a cloud of powder over the entire street. The talc clouds descended to meet Ti Jocelyne and she was unafraid. A group of young men beating drums with white bandanas tied across their faces were the source. The pulsations of the rhythmic drums increased with each step. Members of their group were designated to squirt mounds of talcum powder onto the spectators. Teenagers and children fetched their own talcum powder to join the onslaught. When the bigger kids ran out of powder they stole bottles from the younger kids. The powder fell at a tender pace and covered anyone in its path.

As the musicians proceeded into Ti Jocelyne's alley, she finally understood what they were chanting:

*"Zombie gade yo. Mwen di Zombie, gade yo. Zombie louvri baryè pou yo."*

"Zombies look at them. I said Zombie, look at them. Zombie, open the gate for them."

They repeated the song over and over again while accompanied by drums and instruments down the street. The chaotic blowing of whistles nicked in perfect unison with the steady drum beat accentuated by a cow bell, scratching rake and an underlying melody of portable sound system. As they passed one corner or corridor, the collective chant grew more infectious as additional bystanders blended into the chorus. Squatted vendors clapped along and merchants balanced goods on their heads to the music. Old ladies found the beat by hunching their shoulders up and down.

In the distance, children ran through the cloud of talc screaming:

"Zombie, zombie, zombie!"

No adult paid them any attention. It was carnival, outrageous costumes were expected. Didoune came outside and sat on the wooden block permanently stationed on the side of the entranceway and laughed at the collective commotion.

The chant possessed Ti Jocelyne and she danced in the street. The talcum powder veiled her hair, face, arms, and left a wonderful mess. Ti Jocelyne wanted to ingest the inviting scent of the powder; it belonged inside of her. Jessica ran into the street with both arms raised for her mother to pick her up amid the white haze. Ti Jocelyne joined the carnival revelers in their folly. She rarely let her guard down and or exhibited joy in front of her daughter. Carnival was one of the rare times where work was useless. Even if she wanted to work, her boss Gwo Pierro wouldn't let her. She had no choice than to partake in the festivities because even the drivers of the colorful *taptap* trucks, shoe shine boys and corrupt government officials were diligently at rest.

The music grew faint as the procession of carnival players marched further away from Ti Jocelyne's front door. Ti Jocelyne and her daughter were doused in talcum powder and a voice manifested behind her. Sister Marie Martine, her next door neighbor, appeared with a look of contempt.

"You can't serve two masters. You will either hate one or love the other."

Sister Marie Martine was a miserable soul with a never-ending testimony about how Jesus had saved her from Vodou and gave her a husband as a reward. Sister Marie Martine once gave a testimony about how Erzulie's spirit used to torment and threaten her with spinsterhood. Sister Marie Martine could have been at least fifty years old, but Ti Jocelyne couldn't tell her age because old Haitian mountain women never wrinkled.

Ti Jocelyne was plain and didn't wear elaborate clothes or hairstyles. Yet her childhood as a *restavèk* working in Madan Maurice's house taught her how to present a façade of womanhood: make-up, neatly combed hair, deodorant, Epsom salt steel wool pedicures, shaped eyebrows and double bladed Gillette razors to shave legs and armpits. Ti Jocelyne had observed Madan Maurice's sisters, cousins, goddaughters and neighbors. Getting a man was like tilling soil; preparation, tools, seed and equipment were required. Ti Jocelyne had served as a cook, housekeeper, gardener, car washer and personal esthetician. Madan Maurice denied Ti Jocelyne toiletries but failed to realize that in forcing her to set rollers, give pedicures, shave legs, and shape eyebrows, Ti Jocelyne mastered these subtle society skills. Working for Madan Maurice as a child taught Ti Jocelyne about the Haitian elite. Elegance was simple, clean, understated and often went unnoticed.

Ti Jocelyne felt comfortable with shaved legs, shaped eyebrows, plain cotton underwear, light sundresses and sandals. Anything more would be to attract attention or impress other people.

Sister Marie Martine's testimony was suspect. Her leg hairs were so thick they could be braided into cornrows, she never styled her hair, never wore any makeup or did anything to make herself more attractive. Sister Marie Martine loved to give testimonies about Jesus saving her from Erzulie and Vodou. Ti Jocelyne wondered what Jesus had to do with her walking around like a frumpy ridiculous mess? If Sister Marie Martine wanted a husband sooner, she should have shaved her legs and put on a flattering dress twenty years ago.

Sister Marie Martine lived across the street and remained inside for the entirety of the drum celebration. Nonetheless, she somehow managed to wedge her eye into a crevice to spy on Ti Jocelyne and her daughter enjoying the drums and the cool pleasure of the talcum powder falling on their skin in the midst of the Okap heat. Her voice wisped past Ti Jocelyne's ear again:

"You can't serve two masters. You will either hate one or love the other."

"Judge not and be not judged. I don't judge you when you're gossiping about the other ladies at church--- whenever they are in front of you, you never seem to have anything to say. Yet, you want to spray your venom in front of me." Ti Jocelyne responded.

Sister Marie Martine slivered back into her hovel. She was insignificant in their church circle. Pastor Jeremiah only respected the parishioners who tithed regularly. Sister Marie Martine was eternally at church cooking, cleaning and telling people what to do. Ti Jocelyne conspicuously dropped five hundred gourdes in the offering basket each week and upon leaving the church often promised Pastor Jeremiah:

"You know, when God gives me more, I will give the church more."

Her pastor loved this display of loyalty. She updated him about how she sold different artisanal pieces to tourists close to the hotels on the weekends. She made him believe that she earned modest sums through God's good grace and obedient tithes. Pastor Jeremiah was a self-aggrandizing creature that consistently encouraged the majority female congregation to emulate Ti Jocelyne's financial faithfulness. If the other women could give more faithfully their church could truly begin to manifest the glory of God.

Sister Marie Martine hated Ti Jocelyne because she lived free of other people's expectations. Ti Jocelyne began each day with her own goals serving as a compass. Sister Marie Martine began each day with the intention of finding out what other people were doing or had failed to do. Ti Jocelyne did her own thing and no one in Okap uttered a slanderous word against her. Nonetheless, Sister Marie Martine had tried to uncover the father of Ti Jocelyne's daughter, to no avail. Ti Jocelyne's flawless chocolate skin accentuated a svelte figure and high cheekbones; the origin of her daughter's light skin and eyes was a persistent question on Sister Marie Martine's barren mind.

In the midst of carnival joy, Ti Jocelyne sensed hateful eyes on her radiant daughter as they continued to rejoice in the fog of talcum powder. While other women would have allowed the bitter old woman to overwhelm them, Ti Jocelyne was genuinely at peace.

The fragrance of the talcum powder unleashed opposing memories: pampering her daughter as a newborn and her work with dead bodies in the mountains for Gwo Pierro. Either way, talc meant tranquility. But there was to be no quiet that day or for the next few days. Carnival season was in session and it had absolutely no intention of being interrupted. The air was ripe. Vendors sold more than usual. People were buoyant and everyone expected a fresh batch of babies in nine months. Opportunities were open.

Ti Jocelyne's daughter was in school. Pastor Jeremiah had pulled some strings with the American pastor at the brand new non-denominational school. She wouldn't even have to pay tuition for her daughter to attend. Good old white Christians in the United States had donated close to two million dollars to build the school and pay the teachers. Her daughter was receiving an education, something she had never received. Ti Jocelyne refused to get comfortable and instead pivoted to the next goal: building her own house.

She had saved nearly twenty thousand American dollars from her work with Gwo Pierro and wasn't sure how to build a house without attracting attention. By watching Gwo Pierro, she learned to act like she had nothing and knew nothing, in order to get everything. Ti Jocelyne thought about it day and night. Even Didoune didn't know how Ti Jocelyne earned her living. And Sister Marie Martine was perpetually sniffing around because it was apparent that Ti Jocelyne wanted for nothing. Ti Jocelyne remained on high-alert to avoid disclosing the true source of her income.

The melodies of the musical caravan had faded but residual powder clung to the concrete sidewalks, the side of the dilapidated houses and onto the broken patchwork of tiles, cobblestones and asphalt streets. In the distance, a fast *rara* tempo band interrupted the regular carnival cadence and ushered a new spirit into the street. It was almost six o'clock and revelers piled on top of one another for the full effect of carnival.

In the crowd was Jean, the son of Gwo Pierro's sole confidante, David. Jean was a tall, handsome man and a couple of years older than Ti Jocelyne. He handled dead bodies for Gwo Pierro in the Pilate mountain shack too. She must have interacted with

Jean at least a dozen times but today he was resplendent. He never displayed facial emotion, but in the midst of carnival, Jean was joyful. His presence surprised her. Where did he live? What exactly did he do for Gwo Pierro? Jean was wearing a red and blue striped shirt with words she couldn't read. Could he read? Would he tell people about her real job? Ti Jocelyne never approached people. Instead, she took a seat on a plastic crate next to Didoune and enjoyed the approaching band. This man had caught her attention. Usually she caught the attention of men and it brought trouble. She was 23 years old and even though she had given birth, Ti Jocelyne had never experienced sex freely, let alone been in love.

A group of children ran past Ti Jocelyne kicking gravel in their fury. A short old man turned the corner dressed in white with four snakes loosely draped around his shoulders while holding the largest snake taut between his hands. Steps brought him closer. His face was painted red and gold. The snakes balanced gracefully around his neck and torso. And with every footfall, the crowd swelled as it followed him at a safe distance. A gap separated the man with the snakes from the four men who belonged to him. The barefoot men were painted in a black oil sludge and wore nothing but blank expressions and crude burlap slivers around their hips.

The crowd no longer swayed to the sound of the drums. The drum beat holds power over all Haitian people; it cuts across gender, class, education and religion. Ti Jocelyne fixated on the snakes dancing to the drum cadence. The four oiled men were unaffected by the beat of the drums. The street was littered with debris yet they did not flinch when the soles of their feet met broken glass.

Didoune could no longer see faraway objects out of her remaining eye but one good look at the men would be enough. The oiled men passed. Didoune exhaled exasperation while observing the reactions of fellow onlookers. Ti Jocelyne trembled when Didoune's reaction confirmed her fears: a *bòkò* was parading his zombies on one of the busiest days of the year. Ti Jocelyne's fears fell further when they met with Didoune. Stories of people selling their souls to *bòkòs* in exchange for love, money or power were not new.

"Child, let me go inside. I'm about to be indisposed in a matter of no time." Didoune said underneath her breath.

Ti Jocelyne helped Didoune off the crate and guided her through their entranceway where Jessica was enraptured in a Jesus coloring book from church. They walked into the back room where Didoune's large double bed laid waiting.

"What happened, don't you feel well?" Ti Jocelyne asked in a haze.

"I'm so shocked, I can barely talk, let alone sit down properly."

"What is it, go ahead and speak."

"Go and bring the child all the way inside. Don't leave her out there. Evil is out in the air tonight." Didoune uttered between shallow breaths.

Ti Jocelyne pulled the slanted wooden door firmly behind her and clutched Jessica leaving the crayons and the coloring book on the corridor floor.

"Didoune, go ahead, go ahead, you can speak now."

"I always knew it existed. They say after getting a spell cast that was successful, for riches or power, the signer was indebted to the *bòkò* and promised a certain percentage of the wealth in return for his services. Usually ten percent of the fortune acquired. Yet, the same poor men who were grateful to the *bòkò* eventually forgot the source of their wealth. Month after month, year after year, some would give the *bòkò* less of their promised tithes. In arrogance, their new wealth lulled them into neglecting the lifelong covenants they had signed in exchange for the *bòkò* spells. Ritualistic baths of mysterious herbs and powders ingested through their skin and noses." Didoune explained.

"You think those men are like that?

"Of course they are and now they are his, to do whatever he chooses. When did you ever hear of an owner not collecting his property? His rendered service was non-refundable and he will surely receive payment. This is one debt that men cannot forget to pay. Once they sign their lives over to a *bòkò* , the only way to break the debt is for the *bòkò* to die.

Even after he dies, most of them have been living without a sense of consciousness so long that they never find themselves again."

"But why come down during carnival where people are enjoying themselves to do all of this?" Ti Jocelyne asked.

"This is the best time to do it. Everyone can see it at the same time. When people tell stories, one witness swears before a group that he saw a werewolf climb a tree or a shapeshifter ascend into the sky. Most people listen but few believe. That *bòkò* came to make a point and needed the entire town to bear witness to his power so there can be no denials. The last person to march a herd of zombies like that was Duvalier."

"What do you mean?"

"That man was a big devil, when he appeared, people disappeared. While he was on his power, he would regularly turn dissidents into zombies and parade them around town during carnival for people to understand that his political power was girded by the spirits."

"But why would this man come into town, today, with snakes around his neck with these men like that?"

"To serve as a warning to other people still indebted to him, remind them that he's not playing, and that they better pay their debts or he will turn them into zombies too."

"But what about the black oil?'

"It's to keep them from burning in the hot sun. They char plantain skins and mix it with *luil maskriti* and spread it on until they are so black that all you can see are the whites in their eyes."

"Why all of that?"

"Zombies are about work. They use zombies to make money. The black oil keeps the worms, maggots and mosquitos away. It's how he maintains their physical bodies in horrid working conditions: cutting cane in the sun, cleaning deep sewage pits, installing asphalt, handling dead animal carcasses and hundreds of other jobs that no one wants to do. The black oil keeps them from getting sick.

"Sick, why would they be worried about zombies getting sick? They are already dead."

"The powder kills their mind, kills their senses, kills their soul but their bodies still function normally--- that is why zombies were first made. They had to find a way to make slaves who didn't want to work--- work."

"This is the first time, I'm hearing this thing."

"The white slave owners bribed a tiny group of slaves with freedom to control the majority of black people. They couldn't do it by themselves. Some of the first ones who came from Guinea knew how to use the plants and the animals on the land to bend the will of nature. Their knowledge to control turned people into zombies in the new world. My generation was taught this, or at least they used to teach, what was included: dried jellyfish, manchineel apples, crushed daturas and puffer fish. They dry these things and grind them together with egg shells and talc to make *poud*. You know perfectly well, we don't eat at other people's houses.

"How can you be so sure?"

"Let me ask you one question. And then you'll see that what I am saying is true. The way people are dying of hunger from Latibonit to St. Marc to Cité Soleil, have you ever seen someone cook up jellyfish and give it to you to eat on a plate? Manchineel apples? Crushed datura? Puffer fish? The way that jellyfish are going to waste on the shores across the entire country. Don't you think hungry people over the last two hundred years would have cooked it in a little tomato paste with onions, garlic and scotch bonnet peppers, especially when hunger is bursting through their souls? Haitian people know what these things do so they avoid them at all costs, even preferring to starve to death."

"Aren't you afraid?" Ti Jocelyne asked with a hint of fear in her voice.

Ti Jocelyne had been serving the *lwas,* the spirit gods, since before she left her mother's house at a young age but there was still so much she didn't understand. The man with the snakes and zombies expanded her mind.

"Why would I be afraid?" Didoune answered "I have never signed a deal with anyone. I don't do people harm and I don't wish harm on anyone. I stay here and I pray to God, by myself, when the idea strikes me. When I don't have, I'm alright. When I do have, I'm still alright. There is nothing on this earth worth selling my soul for."

# 2 CHRIS

*Miami Beach, Florida*

It was 11:37 in the morning when Chris hung up the telephone. He unpaused the video game. He was previously engrossed in a complicated maneuver in Dark Souls III. He could usually go an hour before being interrupted by someone calling about a dead body or missing paperwork. Chris liked his commanding officer, Captain Sclafani because he lets him play video games on the job. Over the last 18 months, his department had several scandals: a shooting where a cop was caught on a viral video beating up an unarmed 93 year old black man; cops busted for accepting colossal bribes from drug dealers and some complicated pension benefit embezzlement schemes. Chris could tell that the constant media coverage, Black Lives Matter protests and federal investigators were driving Sclafani nuts. Chris marveled at how at 54 years old, Sclafani was committed to one thing: retirement. Sclafani wanted to live on his tiny boat and hand the shit show to the next sucker who'd eventually take over the job.

Chris was one of his smartest detectives on the force; he was an unambitious former pothead college dropout from a rich politically connected family. Chris knew Sclafani constantly worried about his knucklehead cops bringing in beautifully wrapped problem turds. Chris earned Sclafani's trust by doing exactly what was required, nothing more, nothing less. And Chris admired how Sclafani defended his team against criticism. Chris was once reprimanded for playing video games by some mayoral staffer. Sclafani responded with a peer reviewed academic study on how video games helped post-traumatic stress disorder survivors mitigate the long-term effects of trauma. All of the cops had to regularly ingest the rotted underbelly of Miami Beach. If video games soothed the pain, so be it. At least it wasn't heroin.

Chris never thought about what he wanted to be when he grew up. In high school, he was on the varsity swim, volleyball and cross country teams, and participated in youth 5k and sprint triathlons at his father's behest. He had two brothers and they were all expected to be athletic by a father who believed that the body must be as well-trained as the mind. School and sports came easily to him; he rarely said much but had a steady supply of friends and girls clamoring for his attention. Maybe it was his wavy blond hair or his hazel eyes, maybe it was his six foot three frame, or maybe it was his relative wealth. No matter what Chris did, friends were happy to answer his calls and were ecstatic when he arrived.

He failed out of the University of Florida with almost sixty credits and crushed his father's desire for him to become a Cape Canaveral NASA engineer. But in the land of the blind, the one eyed man is king. To the other cops, and even his superiors, he was a college guy who came from money. No matter how hard he tried to camouflage his privilege, people could still smell it on him. Chris's father was a well-connected real estate developer and political campaign donor whose two other sons fought over the family business. After he flunked out of university, one of his father's political contacts explained how Miami Beach police officers could earn over six figures without a university degree. Within five years on the force, Chris was promoted to detective and has been investigating dead bodies and playing video games ever since.

Bureaucratic paperwork was the most annoying part of the job. He had a trick. When he started on the job he tried to write painstakingly perfect reports.

He searched his brain for the best spelling, grammar and syntax to capture every detail. An old timer had pity on him Chris. He shared how he compiled a wardrobe of reports: one for a domestic violence stabbing, another for a drug or criminal shooting, and one more for a rape and stabbing combination. With about two dozen report templates, all Chris had to do was update names, dates and addresses on old reports and his work was pretty much done. Each Monday, he wrote his reports from the previous week in order to reach the next level of whichever new video game he was working through; today it was Dark Souls III. It helped him to remain calm at work. The only time Chris was genuinely content was when he was on the beach with his Labradors and his friends. The office line rang and Chris paused his video game with a sense of resignation.

"Yeah, Detective Richter here. What? And what happened. Where is it now? Alright. We're heading over there right now."

Chris found his partner, Rodriguez who was most certainly vaping outside of the precinct building. Rodriguez was funny, easy to get along with and kept the best snacks in his desk drawer and in the police car. Rodriguez was senior in rank and age but never resorted to low-blow rank pulling. Rodriguez gladly allowed Chris do all of the paperwork. Their partnership worked.

"Rodriguez, we gotta go. Just got a call about a body behind a strip club by the beach."

Rodriguez looked up and stopped vaping.

"Oh shit. Gimme a second, I'll be right there."

Chris entered an unmarked black Chevy sedan and immediately turned on the blue and red lights. Rodriguez sat in the car, Chris hit the gas pedal and the siren wailed. It was lunchtime in Miami Beach, they drove hurriedly through stop signs and red lights to get to the crime scene.

The first cops on the scene had sectioned off the alleyway. There was no need to call the ambulance; they should have called the coroner's office instead. The girl had been dead for a while. Bystanders backed further away from the blood drenched body as more cops arrived. Yellow do-not-cross plastic tape secured the area and gave the homicide detectives space to figure out what happened.

Chris hated how Rodriguez never spoke when he arrived at a crime scene. It forced him to speak and introduce himself to everyone: governmental colleagues, ambulance workers, coroner staff, witnesses, bystanders, business owners and nosy onlookers. Chris tolerated Rodriguez's approach---play dumb and listen with the intensity of a hungry cat. This nonchalant appearance masked Rodriguez's emotional investment in each murder. Chris shared Rodriguez's belief: killing women was no accident and that charges like homicide and manslaughter were bullshit. Rodriguez listened carefully as Chris asked scripted department questions. Chris recorded every conversation on his phone without the knowledge of the participants as Rodriguez had taught him. It was a trick Rodriguez had been using since he got his first Motorola flip phone in 2003.

"How did you know the victim?" Chris asked nonchalantly.

"She was a dancer here. I danced right after her on Thursday and Friday nights." Said a petite black woman wearing a ridiculous long blonde wig.

Chris introduced himself to two dozen other individuals and questioned them with Rodriguez within earshot. Chris avoided the body; the sight of blood made him so queasy that his knees would buckle beneath him. It was absurd, a homicide detective who couldn't stomach the sight of blood. Surely the only thing more ludicrous would be a lifeguard afraid of water. Chris held onto his self-rationalizations; he wasn't an ambulance responder, his work wasn't going to save the departed. His job was to find the sick bastards so they wouldn't be out on the street.

"Chris, I need you to look at the body." Rodriguez said concerned as he pulled him out of a conversation with two bystanders. Chris put his head back and stepped towards the body without setting eyes directly on the corpse.

"This is different. I thought we were going to find some form of blunt force trauma accompanied by sexual assault. There was no sexual assault." Rodriguez said while Chris averted his eyes from the body.

"Maybe it was a plain robbery, strippers carry a lot of cash, or a disgruntled boyfriend she recently broke up with." Rodriguez grabbed Chris's back and pushed him in a way undetectable to those around them.

The left side of the dead woman's neck and face had been shredded off.

"I've been on this job eighteen years and seven months and I've never seen some shit like this." Rodriguez said while shaking his head.

The tone of despair in Rodriguez's voice made Chris stare at the lifeless woman's body next to the dirty commercial garbage container.

The woman had a bronze complexion and she was lying stomach down in the alleyway. Her white underwear peeked out from her white sunflower dress. From her attire, no one would have guessed that she was a stripper, she could have easily blended in with the tourists and college kids that plagued Ocean Drive. Even her shoes, were inconspicuous. A single white rubber flip-flop remained on her left foot. The other must have fallen off earlier in the altercation. Chris couldn't make out the shape of her face. Half of skin on her face was shredded and the other half was drenched in dark dried blood. Chris suspected that the death occurred sometime before 5 a.m. A young busboy from the strip club found the body and alerted a manager who immediately called police.

Chris had reached his breaking point; he instinctively turned from everyone and vomited uncontrollably a few feet away. Rodriguez handed him a napkin and Chris silently dry heaved until he regained his composure.

"I'm so embarrassed."

"It's OK, I get sick whenever I step onto a boat. Don't worry about it." Rodriguez reassured him.

In moments like this Chris remembered why he was glad to handle paperwork and deal with the bulk of the administrative headaches. Rodriguez never told anyone at the station about his aversion to the sight of blood. It would have made Chris look like a bitch. Rodriguez had an elegance to him that few ever noticed but that Chris was infinitely grateful to receive.

Rodriguez gave him some gum and sent him back to question the remaining bystanders about the girl. Chris put on the blue latex glove that he kept in his cargo pocket and inspected the bag; the victim's phone and her wallet full of cash remained untouched. At such a crime scene, even if the bystanders didn't kill the girl, they would still take cash or jewelry from the deceased. Here, nothing was touched. In a city that was once the murder capital of the United States, the gruesomeness of her torn facial flesh exceeded the sensibilities of Miami's underground.

Chris directly interacted with about half a dozen homicide cases per year. Nine times out of ten, it was a case of jealousy or illegal criminal activities gone awry. This case baffled him. Could someone have unleashed their attack dog on this woman behind a strip club? It didn't make any sense to him. Chris had two Labradors and had grown up with his father's German shepherds, Rottweilers, mastiffs, and hefty mutts. This wasn't done by a dog. Well, at least not any of the breeds he'd ever owned.

By the time Chris and Rodriguez were done, it was almost 9:00 p.m. which meant they would have to file for overtime. Recent press coverage on Miami Beach police officers' salaries being pushed to more than $140,000 due to overtime had caused a flurry of interdepartmental memos. Rodriguez loved overtime; it allowed him to pay for his daughter's dance lessons and his son's little league fees. Even with monstrously destroyed bodies, detectives had to think about the crazy amount of paperwork related to overtime. Chris drove back to the station to drop off the car. Rodriguez jumped into his Jeep and drove straight home to his wife and kids.

When Chris finally regained his appetite, he was starving. He didn't want to be alone in his empty apartment on Biscayne Boulevard. He didn't want to think about the case. All he needed was some greasy fried food to settle his stomach and clear his mind. Chris sped through the red lights to Miami Cafe 2000 knowing that he would order a Cubano sandwich and a side of French fries. Rodriguez had taken him there for lunch after their first case together and Chris instantly loved the small green pleather booths. Most diner booths were designed to accommodate parties of six and made Chris feel lonelier than he already was. This restaurant had the small booths made to seat a party of two, and in Chris's case- one.

"Hi, Chris. Would you like the usual?"

"Yes, Maria and can I get a malta?"

The waitress walked behind the front counter while they gossiped about Chris in Spanish. They wondered why such a handsome young man was always by himself. One even joked that she had a niece that would be perfect for him.

Chris couldn't get the image of the woman's torn face and neck out of his mind. What could have happened to her? He started googling images of dog maul victims on his phone and he saw gashes, bites, cuts and every other imaginable type of injury. What he couldn't find was what he had seen that afternoon. Full sections of her neck and face were shredded or gone with flesh hanging down to the clavicle. Chris's mind spun uncontrollably. The waitress put the food down in front of him and it took a couple of minutes for him to even notice. He poured some malta into the glass and couldn't shake the feeling that something was terribly out of place.

On the surface Chris was everything he should be, a thirty-seven year old detective with his own condo, a badge and a state issued gun which meant that he could get into Miami hotspots without waiting in line or paying. Some of his fellow cops had mastered the art of miraculously showing up at restaurants where cops ate free. Restaurant owners and staff loved having cops come in after dark or in the wee early hours of morning. A cup of coffee or hot sandwich were nothing compared to their peace of mind. Chris never took advantage; he wasn't particularly concerned with ethics or abiding by conflicts of interest laws but he regularly befriended the waitresses. If he didn't pay, it meant no tip. They were doing the best they could to feed their families and he didn't mind paying for his sandwich and leaving a generous tip.

The condo was a gift from his parents after he made detective. They were expecting him to bring home a serious girlfriend but he never did. Chris had lots of women interested in him and he dated some of them. They were pretty and worked as teachers, personal trainers, social workers or attorneys around Miami. But when no one was around, the girl he thought about was a Haitian girl from high school, Sabine. She was smart, elegant, sophisticated and beautiful, in a unique way. When she spoke, she said the most outlandish yet insightful things. In quiet moments like these, when his heart was full of grief and despair, he read through her Facebook page until his eyes were numb. She was different now. Maybe it was motherhood or marriage or adult responsibilities but somehow, she had changed. He didn't want to be with her again, but knew that she had been his soulmate. Where he was athletic, she was clumsy;

where he was uninspired, she was ambitious; where she was assertive, he was laid back; where he was patient, she managed to get worked up over nothing. She was the ying to his yang. Male to female, black to white, fighter to pacifist and everything else there could be. Years later, he regretted not telling her how she broadened his outlook on life at such a young age. His family was liberal, but not that liberal. While his grandmother was still alive, when he was in high school, dating a black girl would have been too much. He hated his inability to speak up, to say what he thought, how he always took the path of least resistance. They were Facebook friends; he saw her children, her husband, and her new life and wondered.

He finished up his food. Chris left a twenty dollar bill on the table. The only thing left to do was sleep this horrible day away.

As he put his car in drive, he received a call on his work phone. It was from one of the strip club staffers he had questioned earlier. It was almost midnight and his shift at the strip club was about to end. He was afraid and wanted to speak in person. Chris used a soothing tone to calm him down.

"I'll meet you in front of the Publix at Shore. They should be closed right now and no one will see us." Chris said while putting his car in reverse.

The best witnesses could lose their nerve and decide to say nothing at all. He immediately sped down Biscayne Boulevard and wondered what couldn't wait until tomorrow morning. The woman's mauled faced filled Chris's head. He was barely paying attention to the other cars on the road. The driver in the white Mazda next to him honked obnoxiously because Chris had entered the wrong lane. A blazing honking session brought Chris's attention back to the road.

As he was about to pull into the parking lot, he recognized the tall skinny Dominican security manager he had interviewed earlier that day. Chris lowered his window.

"I think you're looking for me." Chris said softly.

Alberto walked around and opened the passenger door and took a seat.

"Listen, I don't want nobody to know that I was talking to you. I work security over at the club and over the last three months they've been changing the girls more often. Girls who would work there would just stop showing up, and then the managers, promoters and DJ's start calling the strippers that are off-duty because girls weren't showing up." Alberto said hurriedly.

"Maybe they quit. That happens all the time. If McDonalds or Burger King hires a new asshole manager, all of a sudden staff start dropping off like flies. That happens everywhere, trust me, hospitals, law firms, and even strip clubs. An asshole manager will make even the best and strongest people quit."

"It's not that though, the manager been there forever and he's not an asshole. He's friendly, I mean too friendly. He lets the girls keep more of their money, calls and pays for taxis, and gives them free drugs. I've seen girls get strung out on drugs before, but I don't know, he turns them out real quick, like in less than two weeks. The girls will be all smiles, and the next week, she won't remember anyone, not other dancers, DJ's or club staff, like me. Sorta like they're in a trance or something."

"But you said they were showing up for work" Chris said unconvinced.

"Yes, they show up for work, but their eyes, their faces are empty like. And when Nissar, the manager, tells them to put a smile on their face and dance, they hopped to it without missing a beat."

"How many girls would you say stopped coming into the club over the last three months?" Chris asked.

"Oh God, I don't know, everyday night, ugh, we have about two dozen different girls dancing. Usually a new girl is premiered once or twice a week. Since the girls started disappearing, I wanna say they've been bringing in new girls four-five times a week. God, I think at least, what, twenty different girls stopped showing up." Alberto said

"And you think, this guy Nissar is behind it?"

"I don't know if he's behind it, but whenever the girls get that empty look on their faces, Nissar is the one who gives them commands and shit."

"But the girl last night, she didn't go missing."

"She was one of the new girls. I don't even think she used drugs or even drank. Sandra was super low-key, minded her business and got her money."

"Did you see Nissar with her?"

"Dude, I'm telling you, Nissar be with all of dem girls, all the time. Sure. Listen, we both know that strip club owners get their dicks wet anytime they want. That's not the issue. But paying for taxis, giving them free drugs all the time? Nah, men usually lose interest after they hit it. Nissar kept up the freebies day in and day out, until they just stopped showing up. It was too much. No guy does that for all the chicks they already fucked."

"It sounds like a harem to me."

"You know what, I thought that too, Nissar is one of those Haitian Arabs."

Chris glanced at the dashboard and realized it was almost 2:00 a.m. and knew that the key to keeping an informant on board was to end the conversation before they were exhausted.

"I appreciate you speaking to me. Feel free to reach out if anything else comes to mind."

"Ok. Lemme go. I'm beyond tired and I gotta try to get some sleep." Alberto gave Chris a black guy handshake before returning to his blue Nissan Maxima.

Chris thought about Nissar. He remembered talking to him and had recorded their conversation, as he did with all his conversations. Chris tried to recollect his first impression of Nissar. Nissar was in a genuine state of shock over the girl. He was stuttering, some words came out that weren't in English, he provided Chris with the deceased's work file so that the police could contact any next of kin. Nissar was courteous and helpful. Chris wondered about what he wasn't sharing. Without listening to the recording, Chris could remember Nissar asking over and over again:

"Where did all of this blood come from? Where did all of this blood come from?"

Chris drove home on the empty Miami streets. Past 2:00 a.m. on a Tuesday, the college kids and tourists were barely noticeable and older locals were fast asleep. Chris loved the bend on MacArthur Causeway. The night lights framed the buildings and reminded him why he loved his hometown. During the day, he'd be stuck in traffic doing some of his best thinking. This early in the morning, the road was clear and it would take less than ten minutes to get home.

The girl mauled in the back of the street was too preppy, too clean and out of place. Chris recognized that he would have to review the toxicology report with excruciating detail. Normally, the toxicology was a distant after thought in his department; severe gunshots and stabbings made it easy to identify the cause of death. In this crazy-as-fuck case where the victim's face and neck were chewed off, toxicology reports would become their only solid lead.

Chris was troubled by one inconsistency. In dog maulings, if the dog does get to your face and throat, he would usually start biting down on your legs and arms before he could ever get to your face or neck. Rodriguez found it suspicious that there were no bite marks on her hands. None of this made any sense. Chris grew overwhelmed and wanted to play video games.

His father would call him lazy. His friends would have described Chris as apathetic or lazy too. But that wasn't the case at all. Chris was overwhelmed. When problems were too big or solutions were seemingly unattainable, a spirit of helplessness paralyzed him until he couldn't see his way out.

As a rookie cop, he was routinely called to the same couple's house for domestic violence. He and his partner at the time, followed protocol. They separated the couple, asked the woman for an account of the events, took photos of the residence and the victim's bruises. They even brought toys out of the trunk and placed the children in a separate room and if possible, turned on a television to reduce any further trauma. One of the women was about his age at the time, around 28. Michelle was a beautiful, smart, blond that could unquestionably do better than the loser who punched her in the face. Chris escorted her to the shelter in his personal car, drove her to register her kids at a new school in Pembroke Pines and even helped her move furniture to her new apartment, only to watch her return to the abusive boyfriend again.

When he was promoted to homicide detective, her body was one of the first dead bodies he found that made him throw up uncontrollably and embarrass himself. Chris gradually accepted a deeply rooted strain of powerlessness; he could not fix anyone, including himself, or solve any serious problems. He was a paper pusher and knew how to be agreeable. He made it a point to be pleasant at crime scenes and listened intently, but concluded there was little, if anything, he could do to change the boundless misery that accompanied life.

Usually Chris had his nightly shower and went to sleep before having to wake up and act out the charade again. This night was different. Chris had trouble falling asleep. A nagging loose-end prevented his sleep. What happened to the other two dozen girls that went missing? He promised himself, in the morning, he would earnestly make some calls, and commit to an honest day's work, something that he hadn't done in years.

# 3 GWO PIERRO

*Okap, Haiti*

Gwo Pierro's housekeeper brewed as the first light of the day entered the kitchen. Breakfast could never be his favorite meal. He ate constantly throughout the day whenever the occasion presented itself. His favorite pre-breakfast snack was ice cream. The supermarket chain owner had it specially delivered to Gwo Pierro's house every Saturday morning before it could melt under the strain of the noontime sun. A delivery boy would hand the ice cream container to Sophie, the housekeeper, who immediately placed it in the freezer.

Sophie liked her boss and found it peculiar how he never asked for a serving of ice cream but instead stole spoonfuls straight from the box at random times throughout the day. He wasn't bashful when he graciously called for strong coffee or grenadine juice from his balcony but his attempts to hide his ice cream consumption were comical. He was overweight and it was plain for the world to see. Gwo Pierro was desperate to lose weight but his overeating was a failed attempt to numb a nervous current that ran through his body. The ice cream kept him in his regular good mood and Sophie saw no reason to mess with a winning formula. Things could be worse.

She was fifteen when she worked for the François family. The wife's family imported petrol and owned several gas stations in north of the country. The husband was handsome but useless. Monsieur Claude would get up every morning, shower, douse himself in an unhealthy amount of Drakkar Noir and dress in linen outfits that Sophie had ironed. His shirt button was opened mid-chest so everyone could admire his exposed chest hairs and conspicuous gold medallion. He was obsessed with his own reflection. And for the life of Sophie, she could never figure out what his job was. Sophie knew better than to ask. She liked how Madan Claude was confident, active and made things happen. Madan Claude would describe how she wanted to open a new gas station across town and the next month,

Madan Claude would ask her to help her carry some things over to the new business location.

It was eleven o'clock; time for Monsieur Claude to stand in the mirror and admire himself before leaving the house. This particular morning, he gently nudged Sophie and said:

"Have you ever seen such a beautiful man?"

Sophie had no idea how to respond. She smiled coyly and continued pulling the skins off the chicken quarters.

Over the next few weeks, Monsieur Claude lingered in the kitchen to brazenly admire Sophie's physique while he made seemingly harmless and self-aggrandizing comments about his own shoes or watch.

Sophie attended school until she was ten years old. She possessed a familiarity with historical facts and understood advanced French conversations on the news. She couldn't answer without grammatical errors, but her understanding was limitless. Monsieur Claude's nuanced tone and context were inappropriate. A cold nervous shiver climbed the back of her legs. As Monsieur Claude came closer, he whispered scary nothings that seized her. The hairs on the back of Sophie's head stood erect.

"Sophie would you like…"

She turned to be respectful and saw Monsieur Claude with his pants around his ankles and an attentive penis in the middle of the kitchen. He forced her hand on his sweaty penis while throwing sloppy tongue movements into her mouth. Sophie struggled to get away. He held tighter and tore the top of her buttoned blouse. It was the same yellow blouse that Madan Claude had worn to a marvelous party years ago, grown tired of and had since gifted to Sophie. He yanked Sophie's bra and the safety pins keeping the worn out elastic in place snapped. Sophie shifted her weight violently and kneed him directly in the balls. Monsieur Claude tripped over his lowered pants. She ran out of the house in such a tizzy that her exposed breasts and shoeless feet had no time to care about decorum.

Standing in the middle of the bustling street intersection, Sophie attempted to catch her breath, and as more breath entered her lungs, more tears fell down her face. She sobbed softly at first, and her cry transformed into a wail when she realized that she had left not only her sole source of income, but her home. Despair crept beside her and was about to take hold when a portly yellow-skinned man bent down towards her.

"Did someone die?" Gwo Pierro asked calmly.

"Non."

"Then you don't have to cry my dear, everything else that is wrong in life can be fixed."

Gwo Pierro helped her up and straightened her blouse. An old woman from across the street greeted Gwo Pierro with a metal cup of water.

"*Oh, merci, ma chérie.*"

He encouraged the teenage girl to drink. They walked, not too far away, from the filthy intersection toward the *fritaille* stand where an older woman was frying plantains and *akra* among other savory treats. Gwo Pierro loved the crispness of the plantains as they came out of the hot oil and offered her some food while he enjoyed the first bite. Sophie couldn't fully breathe, let alone eat, but her tears subsided. Gwo Pierro had recently completed construction on his new residential compound. He offered Sophie a job as his housekeeper while the poor girl was wearing no shoes.

More than ten years had passed and Gwo Pierro had never looked at her in a sexual manner, let alone, made a sexual pass. She had seen him gaze lasciviously at cheesecake that visiting friends brought from someone named Junior in Brooklyn. But as far as sex, there was nothing. He was at least forty years her senior and she would gladly be his wife, if he ever asked. He wouldn't, he spoke to her directly about sex and bought her condoms because: *'there are illnesses outside these days.'*

Gwo Pierro had shelves of books throughout the compound and loved when Sophie demonstrated a natural interest. Sophie had mastered the use of the English, Spanish and French dictionaries by painstakingly recording each new vocabulary word in separate notebooks and memorizing them ad nauseam. She admired the precision demonstrated in the six versions of Gray's Anatomy. Each one was different but had essentially the same information. She learned something new with each minute spent with the books, and in a similar way, learned something new during time spent with Gwo Pierro. He was a wonderful boss. He didn't need much. He liked the marble floors washed and the house thoroughly dusted every day. She hand washed his linen shirts, pants and fruit of the loom underwear every single day and changed the white bed sheets and towels every two days. Gwo Pierro wasn't messy and didn't have a wife or any kids. He didn't yell at her and enjoyed everything that she cooked. He even purchased colorful cotton dresses whenever he came across them.

Jacko down the street was dedicated to his mission to have sex with Sophie. They had had sex once a couple of years ago using one of the condoms provided by Gwo Pierro and he was like a greedy guest pushing for seconds. Jacko was lighthearted and friendly but Sophie hated his lack of ambition and inability to think about his next move. All he thought about was getting his fill of rice and beans and trying to dip his *gigit* in something wet.

Gwo Pierro, on the other hand, was worldly, wise and well-read. What she admired most about Gwo Pierro was his capacity to make everyone feel special while simultaneously leveraging confidences to advance his own self-interest. It was beautiful. He had the ability to be nice but devastatingly ambitious. If someone wasn't paying attention they could miss how

Gwo Pierro orchestrated the actions of so many. He helped the *taptap* truck driver buy his vehicle on credit from one of his old school friends. Gwo Pierro owned a huge *tête boeuf* Toyota truck and never needed the *taptap* truck, yet the *taptap* truck driver went a clear five minutes out of his way on the off chance that Sophie needed to go to the market on Gwo Pierro's behalf. Every morning he honked three times and waited until Sophie waved from the balcony:

"The big boss doesn't need anything today. We'll see you tomorrow."

The same went for the fish woman, the meat patty merchant, the shoe shine boy, the pork seller, the brick layer, the cell phone shop owner and countless others. Gwo Pierro galvanized his influence by providing favors without expecting anything in return. He was inconspicuously the richest man in Okap; he spoke flawless Parisian French but preferred to speak Creole with everyone he met. He wasn't afflicted with the annoying Haitian bourgeois habit of stumbling through French at every God awful hour of the day.

Gwo Pierro was quite handsome even while carrying an extra eighty pounds. He was light on his feet and had a joke or an uplifting word for anyone who crossed his path. His curly gray hair was only upstaged by his deep-set dimples. He was a striking figure when he wore his white jeans with his white linen dress shirts with the sleeves slightly rolled up. Once a month he got in his truck at seven in the morning and returned close to sunset, Sophie would lay out his dark denim carpenter jeans and boots. He never told her where he went but returned completely covered in layers of dust, soil and mud.

That was yesterday. Sophie cooked first thing in the morning before Gwo Pierro left his bed. Today she would make his favorite: rice with white *sauce pwa* with fried red snapper topped with plenty of sliced sweet peppers and onions. She prepared the rice and left the aluminum pot covered while it simmered. Meanwhile Sophie soaked the red snapper in a mix of pureed scallions, garlic, thyme and scotch bonnet peppers and promptly placed the fish in the fridge to keep it fresh. As soon as he was ready to eat around 1 or 2 o'clock, all she had to do was drop the fish in the shallow pan of hot oil and heat the rice.

Gwo Pierro loved to eat. It made him feel like he was miles and years away from whatever had taken hold of him. He did his best thinking while he ate mindlessly. It allowed him to see through normal situations. Gwo Pierro liked Sophie and enjoyed her company in the house. Sophie had an energizing productive spirit that encouraged him to make the most of each day. She never sat down in the morning; she was either cooking or cleaning the floors on her knees with a brillo pad and a small bowl of water on hand. He begged her to use one of the mops he had brought home; she refused. Sophie hated these new mops that came on a stick with a soapy napkin attached, they couldn't get the dirt out and they certainly couldn't make the marble floors shine. When he saw her scrubbing it made him grateful and reminded him to be extra productive. She was routinely done with the housework before one o'clock and would shower quickly then change into a colorful dress and await his instructions while seated at the veranda table. He loved when she read his books in the afternoon. The effort she made to improve herself was worth more than any money or gifts he could ever give her. After they had dinner at two in the afternoon, he would as on most days, let her enjoy the rest of the day and take a short nap before he headed out for his real work: scouting new prospects.

Gwo Pierro didn't consider himself a humanitarian. He found healthy yet self-assured assholes and turned them into zombies. The trick was to find someone who was reviled and hated enough so they wouldn't be missed. For good measure, he converted wife-beaters and pedophiles to add to his collection. Gwo Pierro figured, if they had enough strength to abuse women and children, then they had enough strength to cut sugar cane, pick mangos, install asphalt or work in asbestos laden factories in the hidden corners of the country. Haiti was built on slave labor; today was no different. Gwo Pierro accepted that people were superficial and preferred to live in a self-imposed exile of stupidity--- he used it to his advantage. He was light skinned, persistently wore crisp white linen and drove a SUV. The rich trusted him with their lives because he maintained a wealthy appearance. Meanwhile, they humiliated domestic servants and street vendors that yearned for an opportunity to bend over backwards to earn their acceptance.

In Okap, people didn't care that men beat their wives. Men sexually and physically abused children and no one cared. As a child, Gwo Pierro watched his mother beaten by his step-father and no one ever intervened.

His biological father had been a middle-aged, mid-level French diplomat whom his mother had met when she worked as a receptionist at Hotel Montana in Port-au-Prince. They never married; he never placed his name on Gwo Pierro's birth certificate. Instead, six months after he was born, his father hired Gwo Pierro's mother to serve as a secretary to the new French ambassador and never told any of his diplomatic colleagues about their relationship. Gwo Pierro received gifts and cash from his father every August for his birthday and at Christmas. There were no DNA tests in the 1950's. Numerous married French, American, Canadian, Egyptian and Lebanese tourists and businessmen abandoned their children born to young Haitian mothers to lives of uncertainty.

When Gwo Pierro was four years old, the French ambassador's posting came to its natural end. His father's posting had ended a year earlier and he returned to grovel before his superiors at Quai d'Orsay to secure his next desired posting in either

Brazil or Thailand. The new French ambassador quickly installed his own people and leveraged strategic contacts by hiring the daughter of the richest man in Haiti to serve as his secretary. Gwo Pierro's mother lost her job and was forced to share a simple room with her precocious son and aging mother in her hometown of Okap. The family cobbled a meager existence through short term work with the local hotel, infrequent tourist groups to the Citadelle and gifts sent by his French father twice a year. It wasn't enough.

Gwo Pierro's mother married a tall, elegant, hazelnut complexioned Haitian engineer when he was seven years old. Eugène brought him a large shiny red apple when he came over to the modest house for a visit. His mother loved Eugène, his grandmother loved Eugène, but Gwo Pierro did not trust him.

When they moved into Eugène's house, he was nice and considerate, at first. He would say please and thank you. He would clean up after himself. He would give his mother money for the household expenses. But there was something about the way Eugène interacted with him when no one else was around. Gwo Pierro was savoring his favorite cashew caramel *dous* candy bar and Eugène glared at him:

"Don't you see the sorry state you're in?"

"Huh?"

Eugène motioned with his widened arms:

"You're going to blow up the house if you get any fatter. Who can afford to feed you like this?"

Gwo Pierro didn't respond, he couldn't understand what he was saying. How could eating his favorite cashew caramel *douce* blow up the house? None of what he said made any sense. He didn't say anything and meandered into his grandmother's room to play with her perfume bottles and scented powders. He loved plastering perfumed powder over his neck and chest. Inevitably, his grandmother would catch him:

"If you don't feel clean, go take a bath, don't waste my expensive powder on a sweaty body. You're supposed to put on powder after you get out of the bath not instead of taking a bath."

To this day, Gwo Pierro loved applying talcum powder on his body whenever he came out of the shower. It made him feel so fresh and so clean even though he was forever soiled.

Gwo Pierro imported pharmaceuticals and exported foodstuffs. He told friends that he exported coffee and chocolate purchased from peasant farmers in Pilate. Some thought he was too wealthy to only be selling coffee and whispered that he was hiding Colombian cocaine in his coffee shipments to Miami, as some of the richest exporting families in Haiti were shamelessly doing. Large wealth hides underneath secrets. False elegance and ostentatious displays of charity were shields.

American custom officials were less likely to suspect Haitian shipments of containing drug contraband and they were generally processed with less security scrutiny than shipments from established drug sourcing countries.

The compound was enormous and his parties were legendary. Parties helped him wield his power. He regularly engaged a dozen SUV's to usher guests back and forth to a private beach or a couple of helicopters to fly guests up to remote mountain plateaus for celebrity studded parties. His New Year's Eve party was the highlight of the Haitian social calendar and he was gracious in extending invitations.

Gwo Pierro detested elitist social climbing snobs but he understood how they thought, maneuvered and operated. His buffet spreads were beyond luxurious, there were extra-large chafers overflowing with *lambi*, lobster tails in spicy sauce, and a fully roasted hog as the centerpiece. The only thing more visibly striking than the assortment of food was the array of dark-skinned models in white bikinis. Each one wore a metal gauze glove on one hand, a cylindrical bag full of oysters on one hip and a holstered bottle of *pikliz* on the other hip as they moved throughout the party shucking oyster shells. Their bikini clad asses and jiggling tits were too much for some guests to bear as they excused themselves to hide their erections.

Gwo Pierro paid the girls well and advised them not to sleep with any of the guests; he explained how to play the long game in order to get the most out of the pathetic men who would hit on them.

In a rear facing bathroom, Gwo Pierro had cocaine and marijuana displayed on silver serving trays. It should be a private experience. No one needed to know what anyone else was doing. Gwo Pierro never used drugs and actually hated them, but drugs were the source of his livelihood. He became known as a drug dealer, even though he had a legitimate pharmacy, no one can ever say they gave Gwo Pierro money for illegal drugs. Gwo Pierro gave away drugs. And at parties such as these, his reputation grew, and during the upcoming weeks and months, guests at his parties would arrive unannounced seeking more drugs. He didn't turn anyone into a drug addict; he allowed their behavior to precipitously decline until they were no longer capable of rational decisions. For most, regular access to Gwo Pierro's special mix of drugs robbed them of their consciousness in three months.

Giving away cocaine meant he never lacked sexual companionship. Gwo Pierro's skill laid in increasing the doses of talcum powder in proportion to the jellyfish, dutera, puffer fish, marine toad, hyla tree frog and human remains, while lowering the proportion of cocaine to facilitate the paralysis--- and eventual mental demise. When it was over, he sold their bodies to the highest bidder. There was more money and less risk in zombification than in drug trafficking.

Gwo Pierro provided large scale agro and construction companies with a regular stable of workers. Owners of the companies often didn't know that their employees were zombies. Unscrupulous managers were given payroll budgets and bought zombies as an initial investment. They could hire out the zombies to work over the course of at least ten to twelve years before they were worked to death. Zombies are good for repetitive work: sowing seeds, laying bricks, demolitions, clearing and repairing streets, acts that require direct and simple instructions. Zombies were incapable of introspective thought. Managers didn't allow zombies to interact with local hillside folk; poor people immediately recognized the zombies because they looked at other poor people directly in the eye. Rich people avoided making direct eye contact with the poor. When owners saw them planting and tending to crops, they honestly couldn't tell the difference between the zombies and the other poor people who worked for them.

His business transactions were handled by middle men in Port-au-Prince. Their meetings occurred under the cover of the night sky and the back of an old van substituted for a conference room. It arrived loaded with at least a dozen zombies that had been treated by women hired by Gwo Pierro. After the sales, he slept at a hotel and waited for a morning return flight to Okap.

This time it was different. Gwo Pierro's contact was accompanied by a tall, svelte, blond man who wanted to meet for a drink. His contacts assumed that

Todd Johnson wanted a zombie for work or maybe a female sex zombie. White people had weird sexual fetishes. Todd thanked Gwo Pierro's contacts for the introduction and gave them a thick envelope stuffed with stacks of American hundred dollar bills.

Gwo Pierro was interested, not only because he was handsome, but because he admired how he dismissed the contacts without hurting their feelings. Money has a way of making difficult pills delicious to swallow.

They arrived at the Marriott Hotel past midnight, Todd's driver stopped the SUV and a J5S security guard got out of the front and opened the rear passenger door for Todd. A hotel security guard in a dark suit and clear earpiece welcomed them into the hotel. In the lobby, they passed the elevators and a colorful Vodou *vèvè* art installation and grabbed an outdoor table next to the illuminated pool.

"I work for a respectable family in Florida." Todd said modestly.

At this exact moment, Gwo Pierro knew that his name wasn't Todd and that he should be careful with every word.

"What can I do for you?" Gwo Pierro said in accented academic English.

"I need a heart."

"What does that have to do with me?"

A beautiful waitress wearing a short-sleeved red guayabera shirt brought a drink menu.

"Would you gentlemen care to see our full menu? Our kitchen will be open for another hour."

"No, thank you. I'll have a *ti punch*." Gwo Pierro said casually.

Todd handed her back the menu.

"I'll have the same." And turned back towards Gwo Pierro.

"In your line of work, you have ready access to organs."

"Well, I don't have that kind of access."

"I think you do. You're selling men to go work in various industries. The mix of drugs that you give them, essentially renders them incapable of constructively processing information. I would like to work with you."

"In what way?"

"My employer needs a heart and in the United States, donor patient lists fail to recognize the importance of sustaining its minority of creative thinking men keeping the entire American economy afloat." Todd shrugged.

"And how does this affect me?"

"My employer needs a heart and you can get him one, obviously for a substantial price"

"You realize that if I cut the heart out, it would do you no good. It would never arrive in Florida in time."

"Believe me, I'm well aware. The surgery wouldn't take place in the United States. We have surgeons in a private facility right outside of Riyadh waiting for the heart."

"I still don't get what you want me to do?"

"You would give them the pharmaceutical cocktail which would kill them for a couple of days. The families cry at the funerals and the entire grief ridden circus takes place. When the body reawakens two days after its death, you will wash the body, give him a fresh haircut and shave, perfumed baths, and put him in a thousand dollar suit. We will have a forged passport and a beautiful Haitian-born Syrian woman accompany him on the flight to Saudi Arabia. In Riyadh a taxi will be waiting to take him directly to the hospital."

"You want to take the zombies out of Haiti? That's crazy."

"I can offer $1,000,000 for the body." Todd insisted.

"$1,000,000 for one body? Why don't you kidnap and kill someone off the street?"

"We're not savages. We could easily kidnap twelve men and not one of them would fit the blood or tissue type or even be compatible with our patient."

"Then kidnap someone in Saudi Arabia."

"It's about containing liability. We don't want overlap between where the bodies are harvested or processed. The woman who travels with him won't know that the man is under your influence. She will be told he suffers from mental retardation and has been hired to escort him to a Saudi Arabian hospital for a hefty fee. She has an Arab last name and can say a few phrases in Arabic to get them through customs in Saudi Arabia. The surgeons in Saudi Arabia will probably have never heard of Haiti and will assume that the man is African. They were told that his impoverished family was given a handsome sum to donate his life for their collective well-being. The surgeons see it as the ultimate form of self-sacrifice; a poor man agrees to die in order to provide a better life for his family back home."

"Why don't you do that then? Pay someone to voluntarily die and their family collects a big check. Some men commit suicide so their wives can get an insurance check."

"Well, that doesn't actually work because most insurance companies have clauses that render the policy null and void in the event of suicide. But, truthfully, we've tried. And we have offered millions to certain individuals and they still don't accept. We've resorted to stalking suicide aversion support groups; you'd be surprised how offering them money to kill themselves somehow sparks their desire to live. People think that they would accept money to die, but there isn't societal or familial support to make it acceptable. Japanese kamikaze fighters or young Muslim terrorists or even American white supremacists that kill themselves usually have some support from their families and communities; it strengthens their resolve. When we've offered money, it never works out and they walk away. More importantly, my employer is weak and we are simply running out of time and can't afford to wait any longer."

"Why are you telling me all of this? You could have purchased a regular body and gone through your entire scheme without telling me your real intent." Gwo Pierro said with an annoyed tone.

"I need your help in identifying the blood type and other physical characteristics of the donor."

The Hotel lobby was almost empty as a moderate level of music played in the terrace lounge; it was impossible for the wait staff to hear their discussion. Gwo Pierro thought about what he would need to carry out this initiative in greater detail. This man was offering an astronomical sum for a single body. He asked himself whether it would be too much. He didn't bother asking himself whether he should trust Todd because Gwo Pierro didn't trust anyone.

That's the thing about Haiti that Todd grasped. People essentially do whatever they want. The local police and politicians loved Gwo Pierro. He never paid taxes. Bribes to government workers represented the actual cost of doing business. Once Todd said $1,000,000, it became abundantly clear in Gwo Pierro's mind that there was an extreme demand for all types of organs and that the super wealthy would be able to pay. He wanted to kick himself for not thinking of the idea first. He stood and shook Todd's hand while laughing:

"I think we are going to change each other's lives."

Todd got up from his chair.

"Ok. I'm glad to hear that you're on board."

Gwo Pierro, never one to lack ambition, was perturbed that he hadn't come up with the idea first, but he could see the goldmine in front of him. As Gwo Pierro saw it, Todd was all too eager to work as a lapdog for some American billionaire. That would soon change. Gwo Pierro was forward thinking; this heart would bring other wealthy but ailing people into his sphere. He remembered reading articles about some rich bastard that had undergone his sixth heart transplant at the age of ninety-nine. How could the man have gotten six hearts in one lifetime? It didn't matter to Gwo Pierro; he would sell these rich bastards the hearts they needed. These bodies also had eyes, kidneys, lungs, livers, and a host of other organs that could be sold. He could easily sell each body for two million dollars.

Todd didn't know it yet, but his trip to Haiti was about to open a box that no one could close. Certainly not him, and not Gwo Pierro.

They had spent the better part of the dark morning engaged in the intricate details of their enterprise. The sun was distant in the horizon and even Port-au-Prince was calm and peaceful in its early hours. He asked the armed guard to open the hotel gate and joined Avenue Jean-Paul II. The normal throng of street vendors, *taptap* trucks, school children and vagabonds weren't on the street yet. Gwo Pierro enjoyed the warm wind that kissed his face. A lonely motorcycle came up the avenue. The young man wore a faded blue and white striped shirt and slowed as Gwo Pierro raised his hand.

"Take me to the airport."

The motorcycle driver looked at him in disbelief.

"But *Monsieur Blanc*, the airport won't be open yet."

"I know the American pilot who flies the local private planes."

"Chief, I am happy to take you anywhere you like, but the man is still in his bed." The motorcycle chauffeur said reluctantly.

"The man lost his pilot's license for using drugs in Florida and he's been here ever since. I'll call his cell phone and he'll fly me to Okap. The keys to the plane and the airfield are in his pocket. The man has to eat doesn't he?"

# 4 SAMANTHA SAVIN

*Paris, France*

It was well past seven. Samantha kicked off the comforter and glanced out the window and there was no surprise, it was raining again. The French had managed to bamboozle millions of tourists. No one ever mentions Paris and rain in the same sentence. When talking about London, people mention the fog, rain, slosh puddle boots, khaki colored trench coats and the designer umbrellas. Nothing, all these years of reading and watching TV5 from New York, and no one ever warned her about the rain. Over the last four and half years Samantha had grown accustomed to the clouds and downpours, but she still marveled at how an entire country had collectively adopted a brilliant public relations strategy-- never talk about the rain. After living in Paris for years, she no longer mentioned the rain either and required a downpour to open her umbrella.

Beautiful in an unexpected way, Samantha wore an array of black and grey turtlenecks, A-line skirts and leather boots. A turtleneck and an A-line skirt are perfect attire for ninety percent of life's social interactions: job interviews, cocktail receptions, weekend trips to Frankfurt and Christmas dinner with family back in New York. Simplicity was key. Samantha bought a couple of inexpensive pieces each season and was elegant without being a slave to fashion. She had no money to spare and was grateful to pay less than six hundred euros a year in tuition to attend the Université de Paris. If it meant she had to wait in long lines, deal with rude French bureaucrats, outdated tech facilities, the cost of attending a French public university made it all worthwhile.

Samantha went through her social media feeds and calculated how many more minutes could she procrastinate before tackling her to-do-list. She had to finish writing and submit the last chapter to her dissertation advisor. Monsieur le Professeur Goncourt was a nice enough man; taller than most Frenchmen, he had the natural build of a rugby player. Goncourt was at least sixty years old as testified by his drooping chicken's neck and non-conformist balding pattern. Samantha could tell that he had been a handsome young man. He emitted an effortless elegance in his collection of tweed blazers and scarves that readily marked him as belonging to France's intellectual elite. Goncourt's body language exuded a silent lust that made her grateful that his office door remained open during their meetings.

Her binders were full of data and research. At six hundred pages, she was well past Monsieur Goncourt's recommended three hundred page dissertation length. He repeatedly tried to convince her that scientific dissertations relied more upon quantitative data and that she should synthesize her research findings and laboratory results then mercilessly expunge run-on sentences, witness narratives and media accounts. Succinct sentences were better than winding word windmills, he would say:

"Mademoiselle, there is nothing wrong with a simple sentence. There is elegance in simplicity."

As she typed up page six hundred and twenty three, Samantha wanted to write another fifty pages to strengthen her essential arguments. Instead, she emailed herself a compressed file of the six hundred page document to have yet another backup copy.

She put on her opaque black pantyhose, black turtleneck sweater dress and knee-hi black leather boots. Samantha removed the purple elastic hair tie that held her kinky curls in a high bun. Her massive crinkly puffs fell past her shoulders. Samantha pumped a couple of dollops of body cream into her left palm and began to rub her hands together. She spread the cream over her face and carefully straightened her unruly eyebrows. She grabbed a purple wool coat off the hanger, slung her grey leather bag across her chest and left her studio apartment at the Fondation des États-Unis. She crossed the Boulevard Jourdan to enter the RER B train station. Samantha was going to pick up a hard copy of her dissertation at a print shop by Saint Michel and edit the entire document with a fate-determining red pen. While on the train, she reviewed her outline and thought about how different chapters addressed her arguments. Samantha asked and answered her original research questions in her head so loud that the passengers seated next to her on the train thought she was talking to herself.

Does this dissertation support the proposed position? The 2011 cholera outbreak in Haiti exemplified the banality of evil. Who would question, let alone believe, that United Nations employees had dumped their fecal matter into the local Haitian water supply? Why would they? Diplomats are the best at making sure that their shit doesn't stink. They carry themselves with the impunity of asshole cops yet have the social polish to flawlessly protect their self-interests in whichever country they are posted. While working on her dissertation Samantha experienced the duplicitous diplomats. What liars she thought.

Samantha lost count of how many times she had submitted requests for information to several UN committees, offices and stakeholders regarding the cholera outbreak. She received nothing. Article 19, the UN idea that freedom to seek, receive and impart information and ideas through any media and frontiers was a joke. The UN was full of shit. The act of pouring their latrine waste into the drinking water of poor Haitians was the ultimate representation of their self-righteous filth.

Samantha submitted numerous formal requests for samples and reports on water, dirt, grass, animal carcasses and petri dish cultures regarding the cholera outbreak in Haiti. Again, she received nothing. Her dissertation was nearly complete and she never received any of the requested UN documents, samples, reports or forms. If she heard anything back, it was after having written at least six times asking for one report and the answer was a generic form letter assuring her of their commitment to addressing her concerns as soon as possible. she had taken matters into her own hands.

Early on, Samantha refused to settle for the UN's bullshit. Since they were unwilling to make their reports available through freedom of information requests, Samantha decided she would go to Haiti and collect her own water, blood, stool, soil, and patient testimonials. To collect this data, Samantha called her uncle Tito. He had a successful internal medicine practice in Miami and every year, he and his wife went to the poorest corners of Haiti for three weeks to provide free health clinics. Samantha told him about the run-around she was getting from the UN and Tito scolded her for bothering with them. What did she expect the UN workers to say? That their shit had killed people with cholera? Tito grew up under Papa Doc and understood how evil worked. They remain publicly polite and deny, deny, deny their wrongdoing while committing unspeakable horrors.

Tito gave Samantha good counsel. He told her to come with him and his colleagues to the Artibonite department in Haiti. And to bring plenty of sterilized laboratory instruments, medical supplies, at least six igloo ice coolers, and as much soap as she could carry. In the meantime, he would reach out to one of his old Haitian med school friends who was working as an epidemiologist for Health Canada. There was no way Samantha, on her own, without formal institutional support, was going to be able to get cholera samples past American or French customs agents. The American agents were too stupid to recognize the importance of the scientific research and the French agents would bury Samantha under a mountain of paperwork that would render the samples useless. Canada was the way to go; Canadian government officials could be passive aggressive, but their border agents could intellectually grasp that admitting Haitian cholera research samples would be in the best interest of science.

Samantha's Uncle Tito's Health Canada contact e-introduced her to Professor Riley in the Microbiology and Immunology Department at the University of Ottawa. Samantha, in a formal arrangement, donated all of her samples and allowed them to be archived and used by other researchers at the university. For the last three summers, Samantha flew from Paris to Ottawa to study, observe, organize and compare the samples against her hypothesis at Health Canada or University of Ottawa laboratory.

Samantha was happy to spend summers in Ottawa; her Paris studio rent tripled every summer to accommodate the crazy tourist season. Ottawa had tons of cheap sublets during the summer which made working on her research easier. Everything in Ottawa was designed to elicit efficiency and productivity. She would walk down Elgin and have an early dinner at Johnny Farina's or Lemon Grass Thai or work the night away in Second Cup. She found Canadians fascinating. Homeless people in Canada were better educated than the average American. They would ask for money in French, English, sometimes Spanish, sometimes Italian, and if someone said they didn't have Canadian money, they would quote them the day's exchange rate. She loved the calm consideration with which Canadians approached life. She had made a couple of friends at the university and even flew in for the department's annual research symposium every February.

Months away from completing her doctorate, she would never be interviewed to teach at a French university without French citizenship. Never one to sulk, her strategy was to place the numbers in her favor, and send cold emails to every single microbiology university department chair in the United States and Canada. The University of Saskatchewan's Microbiology and Immunology department head had received a Gardiner award last year and their private sector funding was set to grow the department substantially. Samantha sent their chair a spontaneous handwritten letter on stationery and included her resume in the envelope. It couldn't hurt.

Her days were spent working, writing, reading and applying for jobs. She had googled different universities so often that she knew them better than any fashion or music trend that her peers were following. Her last boyfriend didn't last long. He found her boring. He got into her email account and snooped through years of emails and told her:

"You have the most boring collection of emails I've ever seen. It's all resumes, school applications, job posting alerts, requests for information, and letters of introductions. Boring. I thought I would have found something more exciting."

"So sorry to disappoint. But I have to work. If I don't keep moving, I will fall back into poverty. I have no time for friends. My parents had lots of friends and where were they when we were shaking roaches out of cereal boxes? Nowhere to be found."

***** 

Every Saturday morning she would wake up early to wash and twist her long kinky hair with beeswax before walking through the streets of the city. Her walk started on the last street in southern Paris, Boulevard du Jourdan, and ended past the last street in northern Paris into Marché-aux-Puces. She taught English part-time; her African high school students advised her how to haggle at the flea market. Keep lots of one euro pieces and five euro bills in separate pockets, purse openings and even hide money inside her shoe. Never pull out large bills, it makes the vendors less likely to negotiate and attracts ever present Parisian pickpockets.

The RER B train arrived at the Saint Michel station. Samantha skipped off the escalator and into the print shop. She placed an orange fifty euro banknote on the counter. Change and spiral bound dissertation in hand, she walked over to Bibliothèque Sainte Genevieve. During procrastination sessions, she marveled at the French university system's shared library. She got to see conservative douchebags from Université de Paris Pantheon-Assas with cashmere sweaters wrapped around their shoulders, bourgeois-bohème writers from Paris III Nouvelle Sorbonne and everyone in between. The large communal tables were decorated with thin pencil cases even while most typed away on laptops. Samantha would normally use the time to add five to six pages to her dissertation. Fear sprouted. She had no clue where to trim her work.

Monsieur le Professor Goncourt consistently demanded meticulous charts, citations, concise data explanations, primary sources and other corroborating pieces of information. During research trips to Haiti, Samantha collected virus specimens in Artibonite; the contaminated water was cholera on steroids. The virus strains infected the surrounding archaea single-celled microorganisms. Her advisor strongly recommended that she sequence the genomes of the virus. Samantha observed the viral infection of hosts during the cholera outbreak; she examined specific viral genes and isolated particular enzymes which permitted the viruses to hitch their genomes into the new DNA hosts. In addition to the science, Professor Goncourt emphasized the political importance of Samantha's synthesis of follow-up data, assessments on the region of original infection, and additional patient and witness narratives.

Five years ago, Samantha's original goal was to prove that the UN had caused the cholera outbreak; it was now moot. In 2016, the UN released evidentiary documentation and publicly admitted causing the

2010 cholera outbreak in Haiti. Her dissertation advisor suggested that she comb over the released UN documents to corroborate her lab research and assessments and contact UN epidemiologists to compare how this viral cholera strain behaved in Haiti. Professor Goncourt convinced her to rewrite certain parts of her dissertation to reflect the UN's admission of guilt and to abandon emotional rifts and demonstrate a modicum of reflective distance required of serious scholarship. There were gaps in her research and she needed to double-check her sources in Haiti. Samantha had to call her uncle who lived in Miami; he was her conduit into the medical communities in Haiti. The prospect of spending a few days in Miami on the way to Haiti lifted her spirits.

# 5 TI JOCELYNE

*Pilate, Haiti*

Ti Jocelyne used a tattered silk scarf to wipe the sweat off her neck while swatting the mosquitos zinging in her left ear. She climbed the crooked stairs and hurdled over the gap caused by a missing step. When she reached the top of the landing, she bent over and inspected the eyes of the goat tied to the lemon tree. She needed to prepare a treatment for it before next Saturday arrived unannounced.

Ti Jocelyne never liked this Pilate meadow. Ti Jocelyne desperately wanted to learn about the world and ushered every ounce of her life force into sending her daughter to school, so she could have a fighting chance. Only twenty-three, her last seven years of work merited a postgraduate degree in funeral services.

She entered the small faded thatched house. The dirt floor was tightly compressed and left a faint dusting around her ankles with each step. Ti Jocelyne examined the naked body of the young man. His was not a natural death. It was easy to assess by checking the cadaver, but in this case, she had spoken to him. She pulled a long piece of cheesecloth from the *djakout* bag that hung over her left hip and grabbed the sheathed machete that swayed off the other hip. She cut the cloth in half, turned toward the body and settled on her slender knees. Ti Jocelyne tied the cloth underneath his jawline, past his cheeks and around his temples until both pieces of cloth formed a knot on the top of his head.

Humble supplies waited in the corner of the room: a coconut shell with a single cotton ball burning in a puddle of *luil maskriti ,* was guarded by two bottles of rhum Barbancourt, a broad brimmed straw hat with jars of brown and white powders, a tobacco pipe, and a bottle of sparkling water.

Ti Jocelyne soaked another piece of cloth in *luil maskriti* and cleaned the eyes, ears, mouth, fingers and toenails on the dead body. She gave the body a full bath with another towel that was drenched in a mixture of leaves, herbs and brownish powders. She positioned a wooden bowl of a talcum jumble at the feet of dead body. Ti Jocelyne gulped a mouthful of rhum and while still holding the rhum bottle under her left arm; she spat out some rhum to the right of the body. She switched the rhum bottle to under her right armpit and spat out rhum to the left side of the body. Ti Jocelyne completed her litany and left the makeshift sepulcher as quietly as she came.

Locals believed the *lwas* were especially active in these parts. The meadow had long been cursed and even though the trees grew a marvelous shade of green, the ground seemed to safeguard a subtle sallow shade. People avoided the bend around the corner from the river because it had been designated as witches' corner. But Ti Jocelyne wouldn't describe herself as a witch. She went to the evangelical church services because she needed all the help she could get; be it from Good God, Jesus, Papa Legba, Baron Samedi, Erzulie Dantor and anyone else who cared to listen. A pink rabbit's foot and a green troll doll were also stationed in her closet because someone once said they brought good luck. During church service, she sang faithfully from the *chants d'esperance* hymnal; it was the soothing part of her week.

While seated, she noticed her six year old daughter, Jessica, trying to read. It was a thin colorful book with drawings in small boxes on every page, unlike any book she had ever seen. Ti Jocelyne picked it out of a pile of garbage near the market last week. She didn't know how to read but Ti Jocelyne found the images of the flying brown woman with aluminum hair and silver eyes captivating. The woman had the same caramel complexion as her daughter. Ti Jocelyne loved how the brown woman flew among the clouds without fear. Her heart's desire was for her daughter to challenge the world with the same regard. Her daughter solidified her commitment to going to church faithfully. After all, Pastor Jeremiah had pulled the strings for Jessica to attend the new born-again school.

Ti Jocelyne didn't understand the difference between the schools in Okap. She had never stepped foot in one. Her mother fell gravely ill when she was seven years old in Pilate. Ti Jocelyne spent six months asking neighbors for food and taking care of her mother. After her mother died, a neighbor dropped her on the doorstep of her mother's nineteen year old brother who was on his way to cut sugar cane in the Dominican Republic. He had no idea what to do with Ti Jocelyne. Another neighbor suggested that she could work for a wealthy family in Okap in exchange for room and board. She would even be allowed to attend the local public school.

When Ti Jocelyne arrived in that strange new house, the people didn't look anything like her, her dead mother, her uncle or any of the people who lived in the mountains. Ti Jocelyne's coarse curly hair boldly defied gravity; their hair held no spirit and fell timidly behind them. Their skin was the color of freshly baked codfish patties sold on the street. The floors were cold hard shiny slabs that she had never stepped foot on before. When she entered further into the front room, a woman came out to meet her. She had never seen a woman wear such a frightful face. Her sick mother had carried warm smiles. The woman's voice shrieked with an unfamiliar pitch while she spoke to her uncle. A voice deep inside her warned of the trouble to come.

When her uncle left, Ti Jocelyne conjured the courage to peek into the woman's eyes. Ti Jocelyne had never seen eyes like that before; they resembled the tiny limes she sliced and arranged on her mother's forehead to fight the forlorn fever. The woman grabbed Ti Jocelyne's hand and steered her into the kitchen. She threw the flour sack filled with Ti Jocelyne's meager belongings into the corner behind the large garbage bin. Madan Maurice, as the green-eyed woman was called by her uncle, informed her that she would clean the floor, scrub the pots, water the plants, and other easy household tasks. Ti Jocelyne stood on a large wooden box rubbing a crumpled ball of aluminum foil against sand to scrub a pot which was almost bigger than the little girl. She loved the cool water flowing on her skin. She had never seen water run so freely. It was magical.

Ti Jocelyne lifted water in and out of the pot in utter amazement. She hadn't had anything to drink since leaving her mother's room early that morning. Ti Jocelyne cupped her tiny hands and brought the water to her lips. It tasted sweet and she exhaled a calm breath from deep within her soul. As she was about to extend her little hands to take another drink, a yellow arm rushed towards the side of her head. Ti Jocelyne's diminutive frame fell to the floor. Tears staggered from her sparrow-like face. Madan Maurice pinched a leather whip off the wall and gave Ti Jocelyne three strikes to the back while instructing her to wash the rest of the pots.

"Instead of being thankful for a home, you're ungratefully crying in my house. No one wants you. No one will take a child without a mother, a little *sans manman,* into their house, with bad luck attached to you."

The tiny weak girl stood with tears running down her face and scrubbed the heavy pot once more. This scene would be repeated at least a hundred times before Ti Jocelyne reached the age of 10. No matter how fast she cleaned, or how diligently she scrubbed, it was never enough for Madan Maurice.

Breakfast was the easiest part of the day; and the only time rice and beans weren't prominently on display. Ti Jocelyne beat the rooster's crow to prepare a pot of cinnamon oatmeal porridge, toasted bread loaded with spicy peanut butter and ginger tea for Madan Maurice. At quarter to eight, Monsieur Maurice came downstairs with the promptness of a former military officer. Two flaky beef patties, a cup of black coffee and a small sugar bowl waited for him at the head of the table. Ti Jocelyne was like the green *zandolit* lizards that climbed up and down the walls of the house throughout the day-- not worthy of his time or consideration.

"Yes and be sure to tell her that we will see them next weekend." Madan Maurice said in a rehearsed voice on the telephone.

Their sullen thirteen year old son, Jacko, descended the steps in a well starched blue button downed shirt and a Jansport full of books. Ti Jocelyne placed a plate of spaghetti with chopped onions and hot dogs in front of him. It was his favorite. Jacko loved spaghetti for breakfast, it made him feel American. He was born in Miami, held American citizenship but had only been there twice. Ti Jocelyne disappeared as Madan Maurice's footsteps approached to inspect the breakfast service.

Monsieur Maurice closed his book and prepared to leave for the bank. He arrived early to reprimand office latecomers. He clutched the handle to the front door and Jacko interrupted:

"Papa, would you be able to give me the money for my school project? I'm supposed to build a radio controlled flying frame and Micky's father is going to Miami this weekend. I have to give him the money before he leaves so he can buy it at Radio Shack before he gets back."

"Why can't you wait? I told you next week. If you can't wait, then it's settled, you get nothing." Monsieur Maurice growled.

Jacko placed both hands to his face and contemplated his impending ruin. He belonged to the science and engineering club at school and needed to make his own aircraft. Ti Jocelyne tried to be invisible in the kitchen.

"Ti Jocelyne, where are the bottles of oil you carried from the market yesterday? We have to get the food ready for later. Don't forget to soak the meat."

"Yes, Madan Maurice. Right away."
Monsieur Maurice exited through the veranda and into his Mitsubishi SUV. Madan Maurice rifled inside her purse and handed her son sixty American dollars.

"Will this be enough?"

"Yes. We're putting our money together to buy the materials. Three other kids are giving Micky's father money too." Jacko released a sigh of relief and quickly finished his spaghetti.

Ti Jocelyne cleared the table and washed the dishes while staring out the window in front of the kitchen sink. She admired the chickens clucking in the green courtyard. As she was about to take out the garbage, Madan Maurice entered to inspect the dishes but turned to the deplorable state of the clean floor.

"Scrub this floor with your tongue, if you have to, I want to see it clean."

Ti Jocelyne pushed a soap bucket and torn cloth around the floor while Madan Maurice leered suspiciously behind her. Being watched overwhelmed Ti Jocelyne with debilitating horror; it caused her to make careless mistakes. While on her knees, she dipped the large rag into the soapy water and wrung the excess water back into the bucket. She didn't even take three swipes at the dirt on the floor when Madan Maurice flew into a physical rage on her small plaited head.

"Is that how you clean a floor? I have you here to do one thing: clean and you don't even know how to do that. Let me show you how to clean a floor."

Madan Maurice dropped a rag on the floor, effortlessly knelt down and rolled up her linen sleeve. She examined the plastic bristle brush and dusted the floor in Ajax.

"You have to get the dirt out and it only comes out with force. When you're done cleaning, I should be able to eat off this floor."

Madan Maurice violently pulled the brush from Ti Jocelyne's hand and dunked it into the soapy bucket to scrub the floor. She scoured the floor like a middle aged prostitute giving a blow job, expertly efficient. Ti Jocelyne remained silent and kneeled as it was apparent that Madan Maurice was adept and perfectly capable of cleaning her own house.

There was one thing Ti Jocelyne did better than Madan Maurice: pick the best items at the chaotic market. Her small frame made it easy to maneuver around tables and people. She had an intuition for fresh meat, ripe fruit and crisp vegetables. Madam Maurice didn't know how to pick the sweetest mangoes or how to avoid the pork worms. Ti Jocelyne enjoyed the mile walk to market. She was alone with her thoughts and no one bothered her.

On the main road near the catholic school, the playground was bursting with girls her age in pale yellow blouses and floppy canary colored bows. Behind the safety of the school gates, some jumped rope, while others whispered in their friends' ears. Ti Jocelyne used to daydream about having friends to turn the jump rope for her.

The church drummer brought the song to a roaring end; the pastor mounted the pulpit and read from the Book of Malachi:

*Will a man rob God? Yet ye have robbed me. But ye say, wherein have we robbed thee? In tithes and offerings.*

*Ye are cursed with a curse: for ye have robbed me, even this whole nation.*

*Bring ye all the tithes into the storehouse, that there may be meat in mine house, and prove me now herewith, saith the Lord of hosts, if I will not open you the windows of heaven, and pour you out a blessing, that there shall not be room enough to receive it.*

Ti Jocelyne deftly threw a thick handful of wrinkled *gourdes* into the basket. During offering, Pastor Jeremiah observed the members of his congregation with laser-like focus. And Ti Jocelyne gave conspicuously to ensure that he noticed her faithfulness. Ti Jocelyne required regular assistance with school forms and Jessica's homework assignments. She accepted that nothing was free and was willing to toss a stack of *gourdes* his way.

Ti Jocelyne first noticed the church when the poorest town's folk started carrying ten pound bags of rice on their heads. They had encouraged her to go to church and get some rice too.

Church was the same and refreshingly different every week. Pastor Jeremiah prayed, parishioners were touched by the Holy Spirit and handed their lives over to Jesus. Ti Jocelyne had done the same years ago and has been a loyal member ever since.

When the church service was over, Ti Jocelyne dawdled home with her daughter. Didoune, old and partially blind, rented her spare unpresuming room to Ti Jocelyne for almost nothing. Didoune's only daughter was a home health aide in Boston taking care of old white ladies, and sent Didoune money as often as she could. Ti Jocelyne was happy in Didoune's cramped quarters; within that space, the spirits of peace, joy and love reminded Ti Jocelyne of the affectionate security she experienced before her mother died. Didoune and Ti Jocelyne enjoyed a rare harmony living together; even their disagreements were amicable.

Didoune was a non-practicing Catholic and didn't understand why Ti Jocelyne would waste her time and money with the Protestants.

"How much money did they take from you today?"

"Ah, I give some wrinkled bills to keep them smiling. Why does it bother you?"

"When I go to the Catholic Church, they don't put pressure on me to give, give, give every time. They pass the basket and if I want to give, I give. The priest doesn't make you feel guilty."

"But they don't give out free rice every month and their schools aren't free. I'm going to stay where I am because it's what's good for me."

Didoune was her sole confidante and Ti Jocelyne still never told her about working with dead bodies in Pilate. People are superstitious. There was no point in overheating their heads with such things. She told Didoune that she rode the *taptap* truck forty kilometers into the Pilate Mountains every weekend to work for a coffee import-export business.

Didoune knew that Ti Jocelyne was lying and assumed that she was having sexual relations with a married man who gave her money. Ti Jocelyne was far from rich, but she had more money than a rural country woman working in coffee earned in a year hidden in a corner of one of their shared rooms. If Ti Jocelyne wanted her to know about a guy, she would have told her already. Didoune recoiled from asking poor people how they obtained money. It was never a pleasant story.

With flailing vision in her left eye, Didoune acted completely blind to Ti Jocelyn's weekly trips and whereabouts when asked by nosy neighbors. She enjoyed her time with Jessica whom Ti Jocelyne left in her care. They sang old Creole songs like *Ti Zwazo Choukoun* and *Ayiti Chérie* while Jessica sifted small pebbles out of bowls of dried beans and Didoune peeled vegetables for the Saturday night stew. The little girl rolled dough into oblong dumplings in the palms of her hands and listened to Didoune's stories about growing up near the mango groves. There was nothing more delicious than Didoune's dumplings swimming through the beef *bouillon*, only fried sweet plantains or *doudous* mangos could rival its perfection.

Ti Jocelyne boarded the *taptap* bus in the middle of the dust filled road. The colorfully painted bus had images of half-naked women painted on the exterior. Seated in the corner was an old lady holding a tied chicken under one arm, adjacent was an older man sucking on an extinguished tobacco pipe, a young woman in a window seat nursing a newborn baby and countless other people, bags and boxes filled the bus to its brim. Ti Jocelyne sat in the second row of the bus and gazed out the window as the *taptap bus* driver made his way through the winding roads leading to Pilate. Small hills grew into larger hills, and small mountains gave way to larger mountains.

The chauffeur drove on the left side of the road even though the right side was available. The road was narrow and darted with never ending potholes. One wrong jerk of the wheel, or quick arrival of another car would certainly throw the *taptap* bus off the narrow mountainside road. Ti Jocelyne stopped breathing when other vehicles approached in the left lane. The driver, unfazed, moved the *taptap* bus temporarily into the right lane before returning to the wrong side of the road.

Halfway up another curvaceous mountain pass, a loud scream came from a girl inside the *taptap*. The passengers inquired in cacophony. In the front row, a handsome light-skinned man sat with his daughter. The girl might have been ten or twelve years old with two long French braids. The bus driver took his eyes off the treacherous winding path:

"*Sa k pase l la?*

"What happened to her?"

The debonair father turned to address the other concerned passengers:

"A mouse ran up her leg."

In a synchronized breath, deserving of the Vienna Boys Choir, the *taptap* bus passengers exhaled a unanimous teeth sucking sound which made their contempt for the girl's ridiculousness clear.

Every couple of miles, different passengers and families would organize their parcels, bags and children and disembark in the same raucous fashion with which they had entered. Ti Jocelyne neared her destination when the *taptap* bus driver ogled her in the rearview mirror while asking mundane questions.

"I see you on this road and you always go all the way up alone."

"I'm visiting my sick aunt."

It was a lie that Ti Jocelyne had perfected to keep strangers at arm's distance.

"I'm sorry I can't drive you any further up the mountain. The road doesn't go that far up and the bus would get stuck in the crookedness of the ground."

"It's fine. It's not too far up. It's just two steps up from where you drop me off." Another lie Ti Jocelyne had mastered.

Once off the bus, she hiked at least three miles up the mountainous terrain with the skill of world class Sherpa mountain guides, but with none of the fanfare. Her sandals never slipped and her steps were steady the entire way up the mountain.

Gwo Pierro arranged for a dead body to be delivered to the thatched hut. Ti Jocelyne was to prepare treatments for the dead over forty-eight hours. Gwo Pierro's instructions were severe: never stay past forty-eight hours. And Ti Jocelyne, as comfortable as she had grown around dead bodies, never pushed her luck. She departed when the ritualistic corpse bathing and treatments were complete.

A brown envelope of cash was hidden in the same place: beneath the crotch of the dead corpse. Illiterate mountain peasants knew better than to steal from the dead. Ti Jocelyne stuffed the folded envelope underneath her right breast. Someone would have to kill her to get the money. Not that anyone would think to bother her. When she came up to the mountain, she wore her worst clothes and freed her gravity defying plaits for the world to fear. When her shift ended, she packed her *djakout* bag and put her sandals back on. As she turned the corner of the hut, Gwo Pierro came from around the bend. She was shocked but pleasantly surprised by how he seemed to get fatter each time she saw him. Ti Jocelyne wondered how he was able to hike the mountain without fainting outright.

"Ti Jocelyne, I need to ask you to render me a service." He said with labored breathing.

"As soon as you say you need something, Gwo Pierro, you know all you have to do is tell me and I will do it."

"I need someone serious to run a larger program for me. You've been treating one body every week for these many years with no problem. I have a construction boss coming up next week to build out a larger house for this work. Do you think you could handle up to six bodies? I don't need to tell you that there would be more money for me to put in your hand at the end of the week."

"You don't need to talk about money with me. Every week, you've made sure a full envelope is waiting for me. I know, you are a serious man and when you say you're going to pay me more, you will give me more with both arms wide open."

"The building will be different and you will have your own room. You'll be more at ease."

"When is this going to happen?

"The construction boss is coming tomorrow with his men and should have it done over the next few weeks. They will break this hut down and build the bigger house in its place. Don't worry about money. I will give you money for the month. And I have a little gift for you."

Gwo Pierro handed a small black cell phone to Ti Jocelyne with a large brown envelope filled with cash.

"But who am I going to call. I have nobody to call."

"Don't worry about people. You can call me. I will call you because we have bigger projects to work on together. Don't show it off at church or the pastor will want more money every Sunday. Hide it. People don't need to know you have more than them. They'll hate you for it."

Ti Jocelyne sauntered down the mountain, and couldn't believe how God had worked in her favor that day. She had never held so much money in her hands. In the envelope was more than six months salary. It was enough to buy land to build her own house in Okap. There was too much money to hide in her bra; she tied the extra money onto the small of her back with a scarf. Ti Jocelyne added *luil maskriti* , to the money packed envelope. The tackiness of the oil would gel the envelope in place. Ti Jocelyne didn't worry about the oil seeping into the money, no one turns down American dollar bills, dirty, greasy or not.

# 6 CHRIS

*Miami Beach, Florida*

It was barely 8:00 in the morning when a pair of mangled bodies were found on the beach. Chris texted Rodriguez. He could be at the precinct in twenty minutes. Chris briefed Sclafani, his commanding officer: this would make twelve mauled dead bodies over the last month-- not stabbed, not shot, but mauled.

Rodriguez arrived at the precinct and texted Chris to come outside. They drove straight to the crime scene.

"I'm telling you right now, if I see any more bite marks, I'm calling the cannibal police." Rodriguez laughed.

"Get out of here."

"I don't get paid enough to deal with crazy cannibals. If people are going crazy and eating other people for some weird next level Jeffrey Dahmer shit, I want no part in the investigation or any of it. Means the world is coming to an end. I'd rather be home with my family."

"It's not cannibals."

"The last ten bodies came back and the medical examiner said they had similar human bite marks, with huge chunks bitten off the faces and necks which caused the victims to bleed to death. How do you explain that shit, Chris?"

"Who me? I have absolutely no idea what's going on. We'll see when we get there."

"Listen, it's some freaky sex shit. So far, the bodies we've found were either working at strip clubs or patrons of strip clubs around the beach. That's what we know for sure. All with the same crazy mangled mauled bites around their faces and necks. I'm tellin' you, it's some crazy sex shit and I don't want to know about it."

"Why does everything have to be about sex with you?" Chris sighed heavily.

"Because it always is, a guy kills his wife because she was having sex with her neighbor; father kills teacher because he had sex with his fourteen year old daughter; lady kills her sister because she had sex with her husband; and a middle-aged woman kills herself because her husband isn't having sex with her anymore. It's all sex," Rodriguez said while pursing his lips.

"No, sometimes it's money or power."

"Men want money or power because they're trying to get better sex. If men could get Victoria Secret model pussy while working at the post office--- the Fortune 500 would collapse and hedge funds would close tomorrow; no doubt about it. Men would chill and watch sports all day. No, men want better quality pussy, and that shit costs money. Trust me, this is about pussy. We need to follow the pussy to figure this shit out."

The dead bodies were either of the girls or the patrons of three different strip clubs on South Beach. Credit cards charges, work records and Instagram posts made that clear. But why this location? That was the nagging question that Chris asked himself throughout the crime scene investigation. The girls all looked different, some were black, some Latina, some white. The only similarity was in the men. The four of them were white fifty something rich executive types, that filled strip clubs, and they all died the same way: their faces and necks had been bitten off.

Chris and Rodriguez walked onto the crime scene and found patrol officers had already cordoned off the area. A crowd of people hovered around the scene with cell phones taping every movement of the officers as they worked. Chris went through the motions and questioned the city employee who found the bodies early that morning. The bodies were gory and their earthly valuables were untouched. One of the bodies had over one thousand dollars in a wallet. By the time cops get to a dead body, money and jewelry were usually taken by bystanders. Dead people don't need expensive things.

These bodies were different. Most people don't have the stomach to riffle through the pockets of dead bodies, let alone dead bodies with flaps of blood soaked flesh torn from the side of their necks. What could the person who killed them have wanted? Chris thought about what Rodriguez had said about sex. Chris believed money was the root of evil. Money could erase problems, make people come near or go far away. When the victims were found with money on their bodies it left Chris at a loss for words and killed his ready-made explanation. At first he thought someone had sicked their attack dogs on these dead people for some transgression. Why attack someone if it wasn't for money or sex?

Chris went through the motions and recorded conversations with different people near the crime scene. Similar sounding stories: they were walking along the beach and came across the body. This particular day, the dead man's wife landed at the crime scene in hysteria when she saw her mutilated husband on a mound of bloody sand. No coherent words were going to come from the wife.

By this stage in an ongoing investigation, Chris ignored the usual next-of-kin suspects. This was not jealousy or betrayal. And it didn't look like a revenge killing. There was something mindless and horrid about these killings. He still couldn't understand it. Maybe it was pimps or gang members. Yet again, pimps and gangs never leave the money no matter how gruesome the crime scene. Chris's mind was racing at a hundred miles an hour.

Over his right shoulder, Rodriguez was comfortably detached. Rodriguez, as a survival technique, had learned long ago not to invest too much into individual cases. When cases were especially eerie, Rodriguez checked the boxes on the homicide report form and got out as soon as possible. Normally, so did Chris. He followed procedure and made sure to not let the crimes get to him. But a nagging feeling told Chris that these killings were not regular crimes. These dead bodies represented something far worse.

As Chris processed the crime scene, his knucklehead friend Matt sent repeated texts about his bachelor party to be held that night at Club Resound. They were set for bottle service in the VIP section and the plan was to end the night at a strip club afterwards to make sure they all got their dicks wet.

"R U coming to my place before we head out?"

"OK."

"We're gonna pregame."

"I know." Chris typed back.

Rodriguez tapped Chris on the shoulder.

"You still with me?"

He pointed to a small glassine bag found about twenty paces from the body. Chris pulled purple latex gloves out of his back pocket and placed the glassine bag with traces of white powder into an evidence envelope.

Chris ignored the rest of Matt's texts while he and Rodriguez continued working the scene.

# 7 GWO PIERRO

*Okap, Haiti*

Despite his affable nature, Gwo Pierro could be pedantic. Ti Jocelyne and Sophie stayed with him so long because they trusted him and there were rarely any other men around. Gwo Pierro avoided hiring men. They stole, talked more, shirked responsibilities and secretly plotted getting more money out of him. He had few exceptions: his drivers, and David and his son Jean. David was only a couple of years older than Gwo Pierro and he worked as a *restavèk* houseboy with Gwo Pierro's family when they were both children. He managed household chores, watered backyard greenery, waxed the car, handled garbage cans, and painted the interior and exterior of the house all before his voice dropped. David kept the house from falling into shambles, yet, he slept and took his meals in the shed and eagerly awaited his daily chores.

David had lived with Gwo Pierro's new step-father, Eugène, and moved in with them when his mother married Eugène. David was the first to experience the worst of Eugène's angry temper. Within two months of moving into the house, Gwo Pierro witnessed Eugène kick David for failing to shine his shoes correctly. Eugène turned the corner of his lip:

"Is that how you scrub shoes? Go and fuck your mother."

The screaming escalated to a huge kick to the left side of David's ribcage, and another, and then another until the child fell flat on the floor unable to breathe. Gwo Pierro's grandmother intervened and sent David to sleep in the shed and didn't say anything to Eugène about the incident.

Eugène was an asshole. He made fun of Gwo Pierro for eating sweets and being fat. But why did he have to kick David, especially over something as trifling as shoes? David never bothered anyone, but that didn't stop Eugène from growing progressively worse each week. He would kick David over trumped up infractions. Eugène's rage eventually spread; he started punching Gwo Pierro when his mother wasn't around. This taught him about human nature. If someone mistreated a poor person it meant that they would eventually mistreat him too. It began with slight punches until it grew to full body blows to the chest and face which left Gwo Pierro on the floor. Gwo Pierro wondered why his mother never said anything. One day before carnival was scheduled to start, Gwo Pierro asked his mother for pocket change to buy sweets and cola from the onslaught of vendors that would fill the streets with perfectly balanced head baskets.

Out of the corner of his eye, Eugène saw his wife hand Gwo Pierro a crisp two gourdes bill bearing Francois Duvalier's portrait. He stepped between them and grabbed the money with violence.

"You don't see how fat you are? Where are you going, don't you see the state of your teeth? Give me that money. You don't need money to hold in your hands."

Tears fell down Gwo Pierro's chubby red cheeks. Eugène was ruining his favorite time of year. Gwo Pierro's mother turned to Eugène.

"Let the kid have the money, it's carnival."

Eugène was incensed that she would consider her child's needs and talk back to him. In one solid motion, he turned and punched Gwo Pierro's mother in the face. He had never hit her in front of everyone before, only in private. Gwo Pierro's grandmother cried and begged him to stop beating her daughter. She expected beatings as a normal part of marriage but this was too much. Eugène spat on the grandmother in response to her lamentations. He stomped into the bedroom and grabbed a huge stack of bills from the bottom dresser shelf.

"Don't know why I ever saddled myself with this bunch of cursed whores to begin with. If you're not careful, I'll throw you out on the street to fend for your own asses." Eugène spewed while flailing his arms out the house.

Gwo Pierro sat in silence and wondered why his mother allowed this to happen. She refused to acknowledge that this was an untenable situation. She tried to convince Gwo Pierro to forgive because that was what the bible taught. Forgive and let it go. Gwo Pierro observed his mother and realized that she stayed in this horrible marriage not because she was saintly, but because she was afraid to be alone. Gwo Pierro promised himself that he would never fear loneliness. Being lonely was better than accepting the destruction of your body and the suffocation of your spirit.

He avoided Eugène as much as was humanly possible in the modest house. Gwo Pierro stewed as he memorized his class recitation notes. It didn't matter what they did, he and his mother still caught regular beatings while his grandmother watched in silence.

With heavy hearts, Gwo Pierro's mother and grandmother headed to the cemetery behind the Eglise du Sacre Coeur to clean the tomb of his deceased grandfather. He had died before Gwo Pierro was born. When his grandmother was upset or worried, she often went to the cemetery to speak to her husband. This time they didn't come home until the sun began to set.

Several years had passed since they moved into Eugène's house and the violence worsened with each passing year. A couple of scraggly hairs peeked out above Gwo Pierro's lip and his voice quivered. Gwo Pierro accepted he was growing into a man. But no matter how hard he tried, he didn't want to watch the World Cup or roughhouse with the other boys during recreation. He preferred to be indoors reading *Les Trois Mousquetaires* or *Le Comte de Monte-Cristo* to being outside under the hot sun. During his daily verbal and physical attacks from Eugène, he noticed something changed. Eugène started calling him a *masisi*.

"Don't you see what you are? Anyone with two open eyes can see what you are."

Gwo Pierro didn't understand the term. In the 1960's, children didn't have the right to ask questions. To understand this word, there was no book to which he could turn. The overwhelming majority of Haitians only spoke Creole at home and it would be another twenty years before a comprehensive Haitian-Creole dictionary would be published.

Eugène came into the back room and knocked down the notebooks and spilled the open ink jar that rested on the side table.

"You're a beneath the shawl, mulatto *masisi*."

At twelve and a half, Gwo Pierro had no idea what Eugène meant. Gwo Pierro kept on asking himself, what's underneath the shawl, what's a *masisi*? Was he a *masisi*? As Gwo Pierro braced himself for an onslaught of punches and targeted bodily kicks, something changed in Eugène's eyes. He sneered at Gwo Pierro with disdain, grabbed him by the neck and slammed his face into the ink stained table. Hunched over the table, Eugène opened his pants and lowered his white underwear and painfully penetrated Gwo Pierro until he was bloody. The pain made it impossible for Gwo Pierro to cry.

"If you tell anyone, I will set your mother and grandmother on fire."

David stood outside the window and saw Gwo Pierro being raped. David had assumed that he was beaten and raped because he was a poor, dark skinned kid with no parents and unworthy of love from anyone. When, from a corner of the window, he saw Gwo Pierro also being raped, something inside him changed.

The next day, as with most days, David and Gwo Pierro played marbles in the backyard. The two goats darted across the yard and messed up some of their key angle positions. One goat even knocked the jar of marbles that David had strategically won from other kids in the neighborhood. At only fourteen years old, David repaired the car, prepared manure for the yard, and scrubbed the brick veranda tiles. Everything that needed to be done, was done by David in silence.

David leaned into his next marble shot. Gwo Pierro was upset. Eugène entered through the side gate entrance of the house and Gwo Pierro's countenance changed.

"What's wrong with you?"

"I hate him. I feel like I could split his liver." Gwo Pierro answered calmly.

David was too afraid to respond. The sexual abuse had been going on for years and David had completely surrendered his will to fight. He had no family and didn't go to school. Gwo Pierro was his only friend. Playing marbles was one of the few times when he felt like a kid. Gwo Pierro was the closest thing to a brother or family that David had.

Gwo Pierro turned to books when the people around him didn't have any answers. His teachers loved him and encouraged him to take their own books home. He learned about Charles-Adolphe Wurtz distilled ethylene glycol into anti-freeze. His formula allowed cars to resist freezing in cold climates and overheating in tropical climates. Antifreeze was essential to maintaining a car and every bourgeois family had it on hand.

Eugène liked his *Cola Couronne* and Gwo Pierro was about to ensure that his cup ran over. Gwo Pierro asked David to bring out the antifreeze that was stored in the shed. David couldn't possibly understand what Gwo Pierro was going to do with it. Antifreeze was sweet to the taste. Gwo Pierro had stepped in a puddle of it while David was servicing the car. When Gwo Pierro tied his brown shoes, the laces and his hands were covered in antifreeze. As he covered his mouth to cough, the antifreeze was sweet and felt like syrup.

Dinner was served by his grandmother every day at two in the afternoon. As was customary, Eugène demanded a tall glass of *Cola Couronne* on the veranda at four o'clock to ease his digestion. Soda was already too sweet, but *Cola Couronne* was a sugary fruit flavored concoction that could mask the taste of shit.

Around four, Gwo Pierro placed a layer of antifreeze on the bottom of the glass, poured the *Cola Couronne*, stirred vigorously and added ice. Eugène was too big for him to fight physically. Smarts defeat strength. Gwo Pierro diluted Eugène's *Cola Couronne* with antifreeze. Eugène spent the entire night shitting his soul on the latrine. Gwo Pierro lay smugly on his bed pretending to be asleep while his mother and grandmother argued in the kitchen about what they should prepare to alleviate his discomfort.

"*Eh bien*, we don't have ginger ale in the house."

"I'll make the ginger tea for him instead." Gwo Pierro's mother replied.

By the next afternoon, Eugène's diarrhea had nearly subsided. He had dinner with the family at 2 o'clock, like normal. Then again, around four, Gwo Pierro mixed the antifreeze into his *Cola Couronne* glass. David brought it out to Eugène while he smoked a cigarette. That night the diarrhea was worse and Eugène vomited profusely. Gwo Pierro's mother heard a loud thump hit the floor from her bed and went to check on Eugène. He had fallen unconscious while shitting on the latrine.

"Mamman, Gwo Pierro, come help me." Together, the three of them carried Eugène to bed. The next day he stayed in bed and could barely breathe, let alone talk. Eugène found it difficult to keep his eyes open and dosed in and out of deeper slumbers.

Around noon, Gwo Pierro brought Eugène a tall glass of laced ginger ale. He went outside, and with a steady hand, played marbles with David. The next evening, Gwo Pierro's mother walked into the bedroom to place a cool compress on Eugène's temple and he was dead.

Gwo Pierro's mother cried not because she missed Eugène, but because she had been duped by another man. She trusted men and they consistently disappointed her. At the very least, his death meant she had two houses, one for them to live in, and one which guaranteed them rental income. She thanked God that Gwo Pierro would never have to be a woman and endure suffering at the hands of men.

At the funeral, Gwo Pierro felt nothing as Eugène's family members loaded his coffin from the church into the back of the truck. They drove the body to Cimitière de la Resurrection as two of Eugène's sisters wailed and made a spectacle of themselves. Gwo Pierro's mother sobbed silently and Gwo Pierro was unmoved. No anger at Eugène and no guilt for having taken his life. David sat in the last pew of the church. Guilt and remorse covered his face.

Whenever Gwo Pierro outgrew his clothes and shoes they went to skinny David. When neighborhood kids tried to make fun of David, Gwo Pierro defended him. Gwo Pierro was useless with his fists, but his light skin and razor sharp tongue caused fear. Gwo Pierro taught David how to read and write; he learned quickly. David appreciated the lessons, but was happiest and most comfortable working with his hands. Gwo Pierro forced his grandmother to introduce David to the most prominent families in Okap. One of her half-brothers taught David how to lay concrete and brick, how to install plumbing, electrical wires, and most importantly, how to deal with people who shirked their bills. David never went to school but before he was eighteen, he was responsible for local renovation projects. Eventually, his work impressed a group of Canadian engineering executives and David was hired to work on long-term infrastructure projects where he absorbed fundamental applications of materials, structures, data analysis and design.

***

Years past. Gwo Pierro came back from Paris with his *diplôme d'études approfondi* in pharmacy; David was a competent and respected contractor working throughout Okap. David and his mother were his only family. David knew Gwo Pierro was gay and loved him all the same.

When Gwo Pierro returned to Okap, he did what any ambitious Haitian did: he opened his own business. The idea of going to school for years and then bearing the humiliation of working for someone else was anathema. The goal is to work for yourself. Be independent.

He opened his pharmacy with a gift of ten thousand francs from his father when he received his diploma. His French father was never genuinely involved in Gwo Pierro's life, but he paid for his living expenses at the Cité Universitaire, airplane tickets to Paris and gave small cash gifts for his birthday and at Christmas. Gwo Pierro's father was certain that his Haitian son would not receive anything from his estate upon his death; his French wife tolerated Gwo Pierro's existence all these years but refused to break protocol and acknowledge an illegitimate son born during a long forgotten diplomatic posting. When his father eventually died in the late seventies, there were no DNA tests and natural born children, like Gwo Pierro, had no rights.

Gwo Pierro's mother taught him not to let pride get in the way of taking advantage of an opportunity, whatever the source. She repeated it to him often when he refused sweets in the midst of one of his childhood tantrums.

"Don't go for zero, don't go for zero."

At twenty-four, he used his father's financial crumbs and opened his own pharmacy across from the main market. Gwo Pierro loved the bustle, movement and rhythm of the market. Fish women with perpetually upset faces haggled with customers, little kids ran back and forth with errands, women's bodies swayed while carrying heavy loads on their heads and *taptap* bus drivers sweat through linen shirts as they brought new crowds into the fray. Gwo Pierro had a knack for people and for making money. He mastered how to be kind and gracious, but he recognized when diplomacy was futile. You can't negotiate with a person mounted by an evil spirit. When a person harbored ill-will, Gwo Pierro went on the offensive until the person no longer posed a threat.

Most of the customers who came into Gwo Pierro's pharmacy did not know how to read. Gwo Pierro, unlike the other pharmacist in town, Jean-

Michel, did not take advantage of illiterate patients to make a few extra *gourdes*. To really become wealthy, he needed to repeatedly glean money from his richest customers. Gwo Pierro never stole, but if they were going to give him money, he was not about to refuse.

His first loyal customers were affluent middle-aged men who couldn't get their dicks up. They were cheating on their wives with scattered mistresses. The embarrassment of carrying a limp dick meant men who normally outsourced any and all responsibilities regarding shopping, medicine and household affairs to their wives, entered Gwo Pierro's pharmacy like sitting ducks. Gwo Pierro prepared ginseng root concoctions, recommended arginine rich foods like turkey breast, pork and *joumou* seeds, and his own special rhum mixture made out of agave leaves, star anise, pokeweed, woody grape vines, clove, and milkberry. His genius was rooted in an understanding of his Haitian compatriots and the syncretization of standard medical practices with detailed Vodou treatments. Whether it was a placebo effect, he never knew. He gave patients some pills, some rituals, some infusions, some dietary advice and they always came back.

Gwo Pierro built his practice and developed a steady following among the richest families and the poorest women in Okap, alike. Quite often, Gwo Pierro was the only medical professional that the poorest ever saw. He explained that their diarrhea was probably caused by contaminated water and not by some mischievous spell. He taught them how to boil their water, wash their hands with soap at least five times a day, and when their children had fevers he explained why it was sometimes best to not take antibiotics. Fever was the body's way of telling you that it was fighting the sickness. His spared no time or attention when treating the poor women, and for this, they loved him.

Gwo Pierro had no wife, no children and his mother passed away a couple of years after he returned to Haiti without realizing that her son was gay. He had built a house in Okap and didn't want for anything. He gave freely to the poor and whoever else asked of him; in return, they did favors for Gwo Pierro. He never had to enter the market. The various merchants delivered fruit, plantains, ignames, yams, rice, oil, flour, and the best cuts of pork, fish, *lanbi* and beef to his house during the course of the week. He was young, successful, educated and handsome, everything any woman would want. Unlike most Haitian men who had sex with other men, Gwo Pierro, did not pretend to be straight or interested in women. He never discussed his sexuality, but he never lied about it either. People who met him had no idea.

About seven or eight years after he established his pharmacy, one of his white French classmates, Claude, visited him in Haiti. In the early 80's, when Gwo Pierro had men come over, he gave his housekeeper a few hundred *gourdes* and encouraged her to spend time with her grandchildren.

Gwo Pierro and Claude would study and have sex together while at the Université de Paris faculté de pharmacie. Gwo Pierro refused to stay in France; they were hypocritical and racist. He would rather be a big fish in his little Okap pond than live on the margins of a depressing Parisian suburb.

After graduation, Claude married a local businessman's daughter and was living a boring bourgeois betrothal in Neuilly-sur-Seine. Claude still had dalliances with men but his heart belonged to Gwo Pierro. Claude brought a new drug that was all the rage in Paris: papaverine. Doctors were injecting the blood vessel dilator into penises and it was giving gay men boners throughout Parisian discotheques. It made them feel like they were eighteen again. It wasn't approved for use in France but Claude could get a supplier to arrange samples to try on Gwo Pierro's clients in Haiti.

If Papaverine began Gwo Pierro's wealth, the foundation of his success was built on his ability to keep secrets. Secrets came as whispers from the poor people he helped in his pharmacy. Local vendors bartered goods and services with Gwo Pierro, his shoes were shined every day, his hair was cut and flat tires on his car seemed to fix themselves. The spicy peanut butter and biscuit vendor arrived before eleven to give Gwo Pierro a mid-morning snack for free; she had two sons and whenever they got sick, he was the only one who ever helped them. As a practice, they always shared any tidbit of neighborhood news with him.

Gwo Pierro hated social climbing. The idea that one person was inherently important because they had money or status was ludicrous. He eschewed social climbing and accumulated social capital instead. Currency, is currency after all. And Gwo Pierro would rather have a poor person offer him everything he owned than ask a rich person for two cents.

His mother had prioritized the wealthy and the elite while working at the French Embassy. It did not prevent her from getting fired when the new ambassador gave her position to the useless daughter of some rich man. The rich and the powerful play musical chairs; the poor remain in the same place. The privileged are unconcerned by people who enter their realm. Any service or favor rendered unto them is expected and will never be appreciated. People have gone poor trying to do favors for the rich. The rich rarely remember, let alone repay the kindnesses bestowed upon them. Gwo Pierro learned at a young age that sharing his favorite caramel cashew tablet with a poor kid in class created an ally on the merciless playground during recess. Helping the poor was a better investment; he gave a little and they returned the graciousness tenfold.

Gwo Pierro ignored the wealthy. Yet, the more he avoided them, the more they noticed him. Gwo Pierro also avoided politics. Politics is about cutting up the pie. Duvalier, and now his son, held the knife. Interfering with the lining of political pockets would get you killed. Besides, power is only needed to do harmful things; the door to feed the hungry and clothe the poor was unfettered. Gwo Pierro gave freely and was the better for it. People brought him drinks of ice water under the hot sun and instinctively used their own straw fans to swat away mosquitos that came too close to him.

Paramilitary force empowered demons to openly lurk around town. Duvalier didn't pay them; instead he recruited male priests, *houngans,* straight out of the Vodou temples. He gave them guns and branded them as secret police. Their state issued guns, holsters, navy blue uniforms, sunglasses and centuries' worth of Vodou secrecy frightened and killed people. These *tonton macoutes* grasped Gwo Pierro's growing power not because of the clothes he wore, or anything he owned, but by how people on the street reacted as he walked among them. *Tonton macoutes* created and bullied spies. They never paid for anything. Extorted goods and services from struggling street vendors was pay. When the local *tonton macoutes* came into his pharmacy, his staff was instructed to give them whatever they wanted. Baby Doc's regime didn't provide healthcare. Gwo Pierro's pills soothed their ills. Gwo Pierro didn't pay taxes; paying in-kind bribes to the *tonton macoutes* and local politicians was its own complicated taxation system.

*Tonton macoutes* couldn't get any information on Gwo Pierro. Street vendor spies and local kids relied on Gwo Pierro and they mysteriously never had anything to report on him. Instead, street vendors whispered in Gwo Pierro's ear when someone was about to be arrested, taken, tortured, disappeared or even killed. At least half a dozen times, Gwo Pierro heard about neighbors who were going to be arrested and sent them a messenger carrying cash telling them to get out of the country before the *tonton macoutes* arrived. The quickest way out of Haiti was over the Dominican border. Once in the Dominican Republic, they could apply for a tourist visa to Canada, France or the United States which was sure to be approved. Only privileged Haitians could afford to eat three times a day, let alone travel abroad. Once in New York, Miami, Paris, or Montreal, those exiles became part of Gwo Pierro's network. The mastery of his little pond was extensive and none were the wiser.

All seemed well until one of the mango vendors came to see Gwo Pierro about her daughter. Foufoune was visibly exhausted when she entered the pharmacy. Gwo Pierro's staffer assisted her into the back office. Foufoune had nowhere else to go. She spoke through a flood of tears.

"He took my child. She is only twelve years old. She's not even formed yet, not even formed yet. Boss Jacques, from the *macoutes*, came into the house and forced himself on my child. I told him he could take me and that he didn't need to take my daughter. He took her anyway." Foufoune howled under a deep guttural cry. "He took my daughter's body. For what? There are plenty of grown women in town and he came and took my child."

Poor people don't have money or cars or fancy clothes, but they have their children. What Boss Jacques had done was unacceptable. He was often in Port-au-Prince and didn't engage in the local street harassment like his subordinates. He provided regular reports on dissidents, communists and non-conformists to his superiors and would travel back and forth to Okap with instructions from his superiors on how to handle troublemakers.

Boss Jacques's face didn't reveal his fifty years. He was slim, muscular and avoided the pouch acquired by so many middle aged men. A former semi-professional soccer player, he represented Haiti in the first round of the 1962 World Cup. Naturally athletic in middle-age, Boss Jacques displayed a great sense of elegant agility as he walked through the streets. His virility and strength were tied to his service of the *lwas* and by regularly stealing the virginity of young girls. He found them wherever he passed and took the girls in the street, in their homes, in front of their parents, on their way to school, while getting off of a *taptap* van. The girls were too afraid to speak, and if they had tried, it would have been pointless. The *tonton macoutes* had carte blanche to monitor, control and abuse. At their inception, they targeted political dissidents who threatened Duvalier's political stronghold, but by the early 80's, they had degenerated into armed thugs that extorted the poorest of the poor.

Gwo Pierro heard whispers about them taking food from the market merchants, sleeping with men's wives and beating up innocent people on the street. The power hungry created the worst atrocities in Haiti; people seeking money could be appeased through cash gifts, but the desire for power made full stomached and well-heeled folk kill. As was reasonably possible, Gwo Pierro avoided the violent actors tied to the regime. It was a losing situation-- that was until Boss Jacques walked into his pharmacy.

"Where is Gwo Pierro? Tell him I want to see him." Boss Jacques said with casual arrogance.

Louise walked into the back consultation office:

"There is a big boss outside asking to see you. What should I do? "

Gwo Pierro got up from behind his desk and accompanied Louise to the front of the pharmacy.

"Boss Jacques, how happy I am to see you in my office. You didn't need to come all this way. All you need to do is call me and I would send whatever you need to your house." Gwo Pierro stated in elegant deference.

Boss Jacques smiled and removed his sunglasses.

"There's no problem, I was close by, and decided to come in."

"Come right into my office and have seat." Gwo Pierro winked at Louise and said loudly:

"Now bring some lemonade, nice and cold for Boss Jacques and don't make him wait for it."

Egomaniacal people loved the idea of staff being belittled with the singular purpose of making them feel important.

Louise took no offense. Gwo Pierro had taught her the art form of stroking the ego of dangerous people. Better to pretend than to die over nothing. She brought the iced lemonade in a tall crystal glass and closed the door behind her.

"Tell me what I can do for you today."

"Eh, well, I have a little problem and my friend told me that you helped him with his problem before."

"Who is your friend?"

"Carlo."

Boss Jacques was in his office about a limp dick. Gwo Pierro took a deep breath and explained the importance of diet, new French medicines, and went through his standard course of treatment for erectile dysfunction. Boss Jacques wasn't in his office for regular medicine. Boss Jacques wanted Gwo Pierro to make him a special treatment because some woman had obviously placed a spell on him. Boss Jacques couldn't invite him to the house to discuss limp dick treatment with his wife around. His wife had no idea he was raping young girls. Gwo Pierro had to do something. He told Boss Jacques to come back the following day and that he would have his treatment ready.

The next morning Boss Jacques returned, and Gwo Pierro placed a needle filled with papaverine, and what smelled like talcum powder on a small table. Gwo Pierro injected the needle into his dick and Boss Jacques was impressed with how quickly the medicine worked. Gwo Pierro laced the papaverine with a special powder concoction. Another talcum powder mixture was scooped into a glass jar. He instructed Boss Jacques to spread it over his entire body, twice a day immediately after his shower to safeguard his virility. The next day, Boss Jacques was dead. Within three days, Boss Jacques's funeral procession filled Rue F as everyone left Cathedral de Notre Dame. Two days after the funeral, Gwo Pierro went to see David.

Married six months with a pregnant wife, David had a successful construction business operating throughout the North of Haiti. All the same, Gwo Pierro dropped a fat envelope in David's hands whenever he asked for a favor. Certain jobs should never be done for free. These fat envelopes funded the expansion of David's business through new equipment purchases. Women have a sixth sense when money enters the house. His wife assumed it was tied to new construction projects. David kept odd hours and came home covered in mud. His wife rarely questioned his suspicious behavior because it brought home more money.

Gwo Pierro needed help at the cemetery. David didn't ask any questions. They walked through the cemetery in the middle of the night, and as expected, no living person was there. Rows of above ground concrete tombs covered the cemetery. Grass patches were choked by layers of concrete and created an artificial barrier between the dead and the dying. Some tombs were painted light blue, baby turquoise, pastel yellow, mint green, and beige; most wore their plain gray color, while others were covered in black and white checkered tiles. Gwo Pierro and David didn't have to walk far into the cemetery to find Boss Jacques's tomb; money bought front row seats even in death.

David's sledge hammer flew around his back and smashed the protruding concrete grave where Boss Jacques's body was laid to rest. He swung a first large swing, then another, and another, until the heavy cover slab turned into rubble on top of the exposed casket. David cleared some of the debris to open the casket. Boss Jacques had been buried in a pristine white suit and his face was a resplendent shade of chocolate.

Gwo Pierro threw two large handfuls of talcum powder over Boss Jacques's body. David and Gwo Pierro lifted the powder covered body without fear. They had both been inoculated against the zombie powder ages ago. With the seemingly dead body flat on the ground, Gwo Pierro spoke to Boss Jacques while David stood silently.

"Rise, I say, rise. Rise. I command you to rise. Your spirit no longer belongs to you. It will move through this world without any rest while your body walks aimlessly belonging to no one."

Boss Jacques opened his eyes and rolled over. Gwo Pierro and David were unafraid; they had zombified countless other bodies before. The soulless body stood semi-erect but it had no cognition, no perception, no understanding. Gwo Pierro told the lifeless body to sit and he sat. He told him to walk and he walked. On that early Sunday morning, Gwo Pierro unleashed Boss Jacques from his grave, still wearing his white burial suit.

First it was neighborhood kids, then street vendors, eventually former *tonton macoute* subordinates, and finally his wife, they all saw Boss Jacques wandering the streets in a filthy white suit. He no longer recognized the names or faces of those who had been closest to him. Boss Jacques wandered the streets of Okap until he was no longer seen or remembered by anyone.

# 8 CHRIS

*Miami Beach, Florida*

Chris loved Matt like a brother; he was fun, caring and defended him when the bullies wanted to beat him up. Yet, as adults, Chris knew better than to hang out with Matt on the regular. Matt was a physician's assistant who smoked crack laced weed in his free time. Chris tried not to judge him but nothing good could come from hanging out with Matt. Chris hoped that getting married to such a great girl would bring Matt peace. Chris hated VIP bottle service. It was a waste of time and money. He would honestly rather sit on the beach with a six pack and two friends. It was Matt's bachelor party and he wanted to hit the clubs. Chris resigned himself and went with a smile.

When they walked into Club Resound, it was a predictable mess: music designed to cause permanent ear damage, dark lights with shades of blue and purple, gorgeous bartender models who never smiled, twenty-three year old girls waiting in tight colorful dresses and strappy high heels, and socially awkward guys conjuring strategies to approach women. It was exhausting to watch, and soul sucking being in the middle of it. Chris smiled and sipped his Maker's Mark double. The rest of Matt's friends were knuckleheads. They wore tight muscle t-shirts, too much hair gel, heaping servings of expensive cologne and sunglasses inside the club; collectively, their appearance shouted that the douchebags had arrived. What could Chris do? One of his oldest friends was getting married and Matt was grandfathered in.

There was a simplicity to Chris. Half-surfer and half-preppy rich kid, he wore an untucked beige collarless linen shirt because it required no ironing out of the dryer and dark khakis from Banana Republic. If that store ever went out of business, Chris would honestly have no idea where to buy his clothes. Chris liked things to be easy. His pant size was 36x36 and he liked how their pants fit his six foot three frame. Chris smiled and took in the scenery while Matt and his friends grinded on every girl they found on the dance floor.

After a couple of hours, Chris, Matt and the rest of the guys left Club Resound and walked six blocks to the strip club where VIP reservations awaited them.

They turned the corner, Chris recognized the strip club as the same club where he found the first mauled girl's body several weeks ago. They entered the club. Matt's brother, and best man, had arranged the VIP access. They sat on the low slung white leather sofas and two waitresses brought out expensive bottles of champagne, vodka, and whiskey accompanied by a platter of bacon wrapped lamb pops. Matt raised the champagne bottle, stepped on the lounge table and made the toast himself:

"I want to thank my boys for coming out for me tonight. It's good to know I have family. Friends that have grown into brothers over the years. God bless. We're gonna do it up big tonight or what?"

They applauded and slapped Matt on the back. One-by-one, they dispersed into the club.

Chris and Matt sat back and grabbed a couple of bacon wrapped lamb chops. A batch of strippers came into the center of the room and offered lap dances to everyone in their path. Chris politely declined. He was all smiles while waiting to go home. A gorgeous Cuban stripper with deep double dimples-- ass and face-- stood in front of their table and invited Matt as the soon-to-be groom to join her in the private VIP room.

In the back room, the stripper licked Matt's face and said:

"My name is Butter because I make everything taste better."

Matt was nowhere to be seen, Chris bopped to the music and enjoyed his drink. He recognized the Arab-Haitian manager he had met weeks ago with the first mangled body. Nissar seemed calm, but frustrated. Several girls left his corner table shaking their heads. Chris didn't think anything of it. A job was a job and most bosses were dicks.

*Mask Off* came on and the club went crazy. A couple of strippers fought over who would get to dance to other Future songs as they were played throughout the night.

"Bitch, I told you, you don't own the rights to no Future songs. Must be out your fucking mind."

"I've been here way longer than you, chick. I called it earlier on when I got here with the DJ. So you can just lick my clit if you think you gonna make money off my song."

A slender, chocolate complexioned stripper approached Chris. She spread her butt cheeks on his lap and was genuinely surprised when he was able to keep up with the beat. Chris moved well enough for his hard dick to feel good between her legs.

"Woah, let me find out white boy can hit it right."

Chris laughed and kept grinding to the music.

It had been a long time since he had been with anyone as the idea of having sex with the stripper entered his mind, a commotion came from the back of club.

Matt stumbled out of the VIP room with blood drenched hands clutching the torn-off left side of his face. The strippers screamed and ran in every direction with bouncing tits and bare-thonged asses jiggling out of the doors. Chris moved the stripper off his lap and jumped over the lounge tables and chairs. Male customers ran outside as fast as they could, hurdling over partitions, purple velvet ropes, tables and anything else that stood in their way. The mob overwhelmed the exits and made it impossible for the security guards to see what was going on in the back of the club.

Matt staggered from the back with blood gushing from the side of his neck.

Chris motioned and instructed Matt's brother to put pressure on his face and to call 911.

"Tell them an officer is already on the scene." Chris yelled.

Without hesitating, Chris ran into the back room and found the same stripper that had been with Matt. Her face and mouth were covered in blood.

With a deep blood filled breath, Butter lunged at Chris and dropped him onto his back. She couldn't have weighed more than a hundred pounds but she tossed him like he weighed nothing, all two hundred and twenty pounds of him. She grabbed his left arm and tried to clasp her teeth on the carotid artery on the side of his neck. Chris kicked her off with a solid leg press kick that sent her flying across the small room. Matt's blood was still pouring out of her mouth. He couldn't talk to her. She had no level of cognizance and was completely unable to understand anything he said. This bloody naked figure of a woman charged at Chris again and he pushed her down. Her strength almost subdued him this time. Chris couldn't fathom how this was possible. He fought her off as best as he could and he tried to reach for his gun. As she got the best of him, Chris frantically grasped her arms. Normally he would subdue a hysterical person with a chokehold, but her incessant chomping made that dangerous. The blasting music made it difficult for him to think, let alone hear the police squad as it entered the strip club.

Cops ran in with guns drawn and immediately locked down the front of the strip club. Two by two, the cops secured the club, corner by corner, room by room, until one of the cops found Chris on the floor in a back room struggling with the stripper. Blood was leaking from her face and fell onto her bare breasts. Already on high alert, the cops grew visibly uncomfortable at the sight of the naked blood drenched stripper. They couldn't recognize Chris in the dark scuffle.

"Put your hands up!" The first cop yelled.

"Your hands where I can see them!" The next cop blurted.

"I'm not going to ask you again!"

"Yo, lady. Stop moving and put your hands up or we're gonna have to shoot." The second cop became more nervous.

Chris screamed out while trying to defend himself from her crazed attack:

"Officers! It's me Chris Richter and I am a detective at Miami Beach PD, I report directly to Captain Sclafani. Call Captain Sclafani! Call Captain…"

Before Chris could even finish his sentence, the possessed stripper stepped on Chris's shoulder and pounced at the second cop. On instinct, the first cop fired a barrage of shots at the deranged woman. The first round of rapid fire bullets went through her head. The cop stood with his mouth wide-open in disbelief. It didn't work. She kept on coming towards him with bloody brain chunks falling out with every step.

The other cop unloaded another round of shots which ripped through her stomach and made her fall to her knees. Butter was visibly weakened by the blood gushing out of her. Scared and panicking, the other cop let out a barrage of shots aimed at her heart and missed. The next release of bullets tore the left shoulder entirely from her torso. More blood streamed out of her, until she became so weak that she collapsed outright and died slowly in a pool of her own blood.

The purple and blue strobe lights were still blinking. The heavy bass in the music made it impossible to hear each other. Chris crawled from behind the dead body, his shirt was covered in her blood. He vomited uncontrollably. Embarrassed, he came to his feet and shouted over the loud music:

"I'm a cop! I'm a cop!"

Paramedics were let in after the cops secured every room, closet and corner in the club. They rushed Matt's limp body to the hospital. Matt was semi-conscious. His brother saved his life by applying continuous pressure to the side of his face. They loaded him onto a stretcher and rolled him to an ambulance.

When Chris regained his footing, there was one person in the club that wasn't either a cop or emergency services worker: Nissar.

Nissar was standing in the front corner of the club, close to the main entrance with a cigarette in his hand while he rubbed his forehead incessantly. This was the second known death directly associated with Nissar's club; the other grisly dead bodies were all found within half a mile of the strip club. Chris wasn't superstitious and he didn't believe in coincidences, but that night, Chris had no doubt that Nissar was connected to these gruesome deaths. He could not explain how. Chris walked out of the front door covered in blood and pretended that he wasn't going to arrest Nissar tomorrow on some fabricated charge. But for now, Chris went to the ambulance to check on Matt. He approached the rear ambulance door and as he was about to step on, a female paramedic wearing a dark cap and long ponytail stopped him:

"I'm sorry sir, we can't allow you to board the ambulance."

Chris lifted his shirt, and displayed his badge; her co-worker gestured for him to board the ambulance without any further delay. Matt was badly hurt; his left cheek and a piece of skin which normally belonged right underneath his ear were hanging off his neck. They wanted to administer a powerful painkiller to dull Matt's pain while he laid in the rear of the speeding ambulance. The sirens wailed during the speeding ride. Chris composed himself at the sight of his friend's blood.

"What happened back there? I saw the two of you and everything was fine."

Matt was in better shape once the painkillers hit, his head was still spinning but the pain had subsided. Chris asked him again:

"What happened?"

"I don't know, I don't know."

The paramedic seemed visibly annoyed at Chris for being there and asked him to sit back so she could access one of the shelves on the side of the ambulance. She pulled out a chart to ask Matt questions.

"Sir we're heading to the hospital and I need to know if you have any allergies."

"Huh?"

"Shouldn't you have asked him that before? Matt are you allergic to anything?" Chris said.

"What, like peanuts?" Matt answered.

The paramedic persisted.

"It can be anything, do you have food allergies, are you allergic to penicillin or any other medication?"

"No, I can eat anything"

"Have you taken any medication or drugs today?

"I had some coke today."

"When did you have it? I was with you all night, I checked your pockets when you left your clothes on the ironing table before you jumped in the shower, we took my car to the club and I even went with you to the bathroom when you went to take a piss."

"That crazy bitch gave me the coke when we went back into the room and she didn't ask me for any extra money. Nothing."

"Then what?"

"I don't know. I was cutting up the coke on the table and she was dancing sexy and shit in the corner and all of a sudden the bitch just snapped and came at me."

"What did you do? I mean what did you say? I know you Matt, you always have something to say."

"I'm telling you the truth. I was cutting up the coke on the table and I looked up and she was making sexy faces at me. She grabbed the lamb chop off the table and started licking it like it was a dick. She was dancing freaky and touching her clit. Next thing I know, she started biting me and that's when I tried to get away as fast as I could."

"Did you have sex with her in there?"

"Sex, I didn't even get a chance to put her titty in my mouth. Bitch went crazy."

The girl appeared normal when she escorted Matt into the back room. What could have caused such a crazy change in her? Matt could be an asshole, and if a stripper punched or slapped him, she would almost certainly be well within her rights. But try to eat his face off? It didn't make any sense.

# 9 TI JOCELYNE

*Pilate, Haiti*

A month had passed since Gwo Pierro gave Ti
Jocelyne a new cellphone. She followed his
instructions and rode the *taptap* bus to Pilate a day
earlier than usual. Ti Jocelyne used the extra cash
from Gwo Pierro to buy new dresses for Jessica and
crisp cotton sheets for Didoune. Ti Jocelyne didn't
relax during her time off; on weekdays, she sold
artisanal handcrafts on the street. Strategically
positioned around Rue 27, she was between Hotel
Mont Joli and Hotel Roi Christophe. She charged the

tourists whatever she wanted and they were glad to put money directly into the hands of a poor woman.

Gwo Pierro taught her how to create appearances. Ti Jocelyne had to account for the money. Selling wooden goblets and cheap painting reproductions, locals pigeonholed her as a street vendor.

When she stepped off the *taptap* bus in Pilate, Ti Jocelyne was full of questions. As she ascended the mountain by foot, the corner of a house gradually came into view. The new structure was bigger than the hut it replaced; it had doors, the façade was painted a pristine shade of grey. Inside, shiny concrete floors and white walls created an unfamiliar experience. Goosebumps raced up her arms when Ti Jocelyne stepped into the cold sparsely furnished house. Six identical iron forged beds were covered with white sheets. To the left, two white machines stood next to shelves of boxes and additional folded white sheets. Further down the corridor, a separate room held a double sized bed framed by nightstands. Ti Jocelyne turned into a seemingly empty corner and found a sink, toilet and shower. Ti Jocelyne never noticed that there weren't any windows in the old hut. The room she rented from Didoune didn't have any windows either. Windows must be what made the new space so cold.

No bodies awaited her in this strange space. She stirred about the house and went through the shelves in the main room: tall jars filled with powders, bottles of rhum, bags of herbs, bandages, metal pots of *luil maskriti*, sponges, layers of cut up pieces of white cloth and dozens of stacked large white enamel bowls, brushes, scissors, knives, combs, nail cutters, and something that had never been made available before: soap. Why did the dead need soap? She would never ask Gwo Pierro for details. If he wanted her to know, he would tell her. Ti Jocelyne sat on one of the new beds and the door opened.

Gwo Pierro entered with David, and his son, Jean. The men placed a seemingly lifeless body on the first bed and hurried back outside and brought in another body as quickly as the first. In the five years she worked for Gwo Pierro, she never knew how the bodies were delivered to the mountain. Now there were two men. Ti Jocelyne wasn't going to introduce herself. She didn't speak to men, there was no point. They would only waste her time. The men returned with more bodies until there were six.

"I'm going to ask you to wait for me outside." Gwo Pierro said to the men.

"Give the bodies more treatments. Do everything you normally do. But this time, you need to shave the men's faces, wash under their arms with soap, cut their nails, shave their hair, do their *twalèt* and put deodorant on them. We want them as clean as possible. Then you can leave on Saturday evening, like normal."

Ti Jocelyne glanced at the bodies behind her and examined the fat brown envelope Gwo Pierro handed her. She was equal to the task.

"I have confidence in you. I won't be back up here for a long time and you won't see these men again. More bodies will be waiting for you next time. You have my phone number. Call me if you need anything."

"Well, I had one question..." Ti Jocelyne stuttered "What are the white machines in the back?"

"Oh, yes. I almost forgot. I bought you a washing machine and dryer to wash the sheets and towels and everything else. Let me show you."

Gwo Pierro walked to the machine and threw in one of the towels. He measured a cup of powdered soap, tossed it in the machine, lowered the white metal cover and twisted the knob to the bold red line. Ti Jocelyne heard the water running and was curious how the water flowed into the machine.

"The machine will make lots of different noises. When the machine stops it will make no more noise. Take whatever is in the machine." Gwo Pierro pinched another clean towel off the shelf and ran it under the faucet.

"Then you put the wet things in the dryer, like this..." Gwo Pierro pressed the start button and the machine generated a heavy buzzing noise.

"You don't have to worry about anything. There are plates on the roof that capture the sun's power and a generator is hooked up outside to power the air conditioners, the washer, the dryer, and the lights. I need you to be comfortable. We have a lot of work to do." Gwo Pierro gave her a pat on the back.

His affairs were in safe hands. Gwo Pierro descended the curved mountain path to rejoin David and Jean waiting in the off-road vehicle.

The washing machine and dryer were so loud that Ti Jocelyne could hardly think. She glanced at the six white beds and dead bodies. She reached for the large white enamel bowls and walked over to the large metal sink in the corridor. She filled six bowls with warm water and positioned a bowl at the foot of each dead body. Ti Jocelyne poured *luil maskriti* , a variety of herbs, dried plants and a mixture of powders into each bowl of water and lugged a huge metal bucket of warm soapy water to soak torn washcloths. It was time to treat the dead bodies.

With a stomach divided into six different sections, he was a muscular man despite his slender frame. Ti Jocelyne lifted his arm and washed the armpits in a circular motion. She washed behind his ears and removed the crust out of his eyes. She shaved the man's face and used a buzzer to make his hair neat. She dunked the washcloth into the bucket and removed the remaining dirt on his arms and legs. Her hands turned in opposite directions to wring the water out of the washcloth. Ti Jocelyne questioned the new procedure. Normally, she didn't wash under their arms or their private parts. She felt no embarrassment, as she washed one testicle, then the other. She cleaned the shaft and lifted both dead legs to reach between the butt cheeks. Ti Jocelyne dried the body with a fresh towel and sprinkled Gwo

Pierro's blend of talc and herbs underneath the testicles and the penis while leaving a dense powder coating over his chest. The body was finished with new steps: she rubbed deodorant into its armpits and a clipper to cut fingernails and toenails alike, finished by clear nail polish. Ti Jocelyne tended to the other bodies.

When the bodies arrived, they never had any jewelry or clothing, other than a piece of white material girding their loins. No shoes, no shirts, nothing that indicated who these men had been. The bodies were healthy, firm, young and muscular. Bodies belonging to the elderly, women, or children were never treated. Nor did the bodies carry skin buttons of chronic sickness or the protruding stomachs of poverty. The hands on the bodies were soft, definitely not the hands of those who worked the fields. Most of the bodies had circumcised penises and she found it bizarre when a dead body still had the foreskin attached. It made the cleaning procedure ten times more difficult. Ti Jocelyne saw an erect penis with foreskin once and it seemed to move easy enough. On dead bodies, the foreskin was glued to the shaft with smegma and refused to move. Penises were an occupational occurrence and did nothing to turn her towards men. There was no allure or excitement at the prospect of male companionship. Aside from Gwo Pierro, she didn't have a relationship with any men. Men weren't to be trusted.

As a child at Madan Maurice's house, Ti Jocelyne cleaned, scrubbed and received beatings. A different life did not exist. Her days were long and tiresome. Her rest came when Madan Maurice visited friends and family. Ti Jocelyne had the house to herself. Peace and quiet. No one to yell at her. She would sneak into Madan Maurice's bathroom and steal a pea sized amount of toothpaste. In the large gold framed mirror her nipples resembled swollen mosquito bites. Her body was sweating more and she did not understand why. Every day she wore the same brown flowered skirt with a checkered t-shirt. The sweat collected under her arms until she slept on discarded rags on the cool kitchen floor at night.

Ti Jocelyne was only good at making mistakes, or so Madan Maurice always told her. She was reprimanded for how she cleaned or scrubbed or lingered in completing simple tasks. The constant insults had no identifiable end. More recently, the attacks were based on her smell. When Ti Jocelyne was in the living room, Madan Maurice would snide:

"Woosh, I can catch your smell from out here. You don't know to wash your front?"

Ti Jocelyne never understood Madan Maurice.

"You can't wash your front?" Ti Jocelyne lowered her head and scrubbed the pots.

Rich women like Madan Maurice purposely kept their *restavèk* dirty and in shambles. They were wary of their husbands cheating on them with the young girls working in their houses. Madan Maurice and her peers did not pay these girls as they already generously provided housing, clothing and food. Instead, Ti Jocelyne was denied access to soap, underwear, hair grease, shampoo, conditioner, lotion, talcum powder, and maxi pads. Madan Maurice openly taunted Ti Jocelyne about her personal hygiene to dissuade her husband from having sex with her. Her husband had a clutter of mistresses, as was to be expected, but she refused to be disrespected in her own house. A line had to be drawn somewhere. It was drawn through Ti Jocelyne.

Ti Jocelyne was incapable of imagining another life. Her mornings consisted of wiping the crust out of her eyes and squat peeing in a corner in the backyard. When it was dark at night, she was too afraid to go outside and instead pissed in a chipped white enamel pot. Most times, she used the outdoor latrine to shit. During her first week working for Madan Maurice, she received a powerful backhanded slap across her seven year old face.

"What are you trying to do? Kill people? Don't you dare permit yourself to wipe your filthy ass and then handle people's food. Where you came from they didn't teach you how to wash your hands after you touch your *bounda*?"

Madan Maurice opened the faucet and burned her little hands under the scalding hot water while pouring dishwashing soap.

"When you wipe your behind and your front, make sure to wash your hands with lots of soap and hot water."

Madan Maurice wasn't superstitious. Peasants accused neighbors of witchcraft because children were falling sick and dying. The poor didn't have access to clean water to wash their hands. Good basic hygiene would resolve many of the health issues. This was the extent of feminine hygiene Ti Jocelyne received from Madan Maurice: clean yourself with hot water and lots of soap. When she got dirty from cleaning chickens, or sullied in huge muddy puddles, or any other undesired errand required of her, Ti Jocelyne relied on soap and hot water.

Ti Jocelyne loved when it rained at night. She would stand in the corner of the backyard and let the rain clean her. She would bring a handful of dishwashing soap and wash as much of herself as she could. She had to hurry, during this time of year the rain would only last an hour or so in the evening but during hurricane season she had more time. Hurricanes start like normal rain until they can no longer hold back their rage.

Madan Maurice, her husband, and their son went to Monsieur Maurice's father house during the most dangerous hurricanes. He had an advanced generator system that could sustain their provisions for months. All of Monsieur Maurice's brothers and their children would huddle together at the family compound to wait out the storm. Monsieur Maurice had no guns in his house but admitted they were indispensable during post hurricane lootings, outages and supply shortages. Comfortable, their entire extended family hunkered down and watched DVD's as others struggled without shelter, food, and water.

While they were gone, Ti Jocelyne was happy. The hurricane meant that neighbors boarded windows to avoid shards of flying glass. She could finally cleanse herself. Frightened, Ti Jocelyne still did not dare shower in the family bathroom in their absence. Ti Jocelyne cleaned the bathroom every day, yet never thought herself worthy of their amenities.

She lifted the dirty shirt off her back exposing a concave stomach and reached for the dishwasher soap. Madan Maurice bought it by the caseload. Ti Jocelyne clasped handfuls of soap and met the fierce hurricane in the backyard. She spread the soap over her face, under her arms, beneath her butt and down to her ankles. The powerful wind and cool water scratched new wells of strength as they hit Ti Jocelyne's tender adolescent frame. Her soapy fingertips ran through her Congo curls until they reached the scalp. Suds ran down her face and stung her eyes. Dirt and pain were temporary. Ti Jocelyne didn't mind the sting. The fierce wind prepared her for whatever was to come.

Ti Jocelyne returned indoors when the vivid winds tossed furniture across the yard. She dried herself with a clean dish towel and listened to the howling hurricane. She should have been afraid of hurricanes but she wasn't. Hurricane season was her peace. She appreciated its cleansing nature. How it cleared the streets. How it emptied that house. How it made people hide. Madan Maurice was gone. It was her only respite from the daily abuse. Ti Jocelyne longed for hurricanes and would often summon the storms. When hurricanes hit the island, Ti Jocelyne was safe.

As the storm reached its climax, Ti Jocelyne spread an old blanket on the cold marble floor and sang one of her mother's melodies. An incandescent spirit filled the room:

*Yo nan lakou a. M ape mande si w wè granmoun yo nan lakou a*
*Yo poko we mwen, Yo poko we mwen*
*Terrr'a glisse la. Yo poko we mwen*

*They are in the yard. I'm asking if you've seen the grown folk in the yard.*
*They haven't seen me yet, they haven't seen me yet*
*The ground is slippery, they haven't seen me yet*

*Yo nan lakou'a. M'ap e mande si we gran moun yo nan lakou'an*
*Yo poko we mwen, Yo poko we mwen*
*Terrr'a glisse la. Yo poko we mwen*

*Yo nan lakou'a. M'ap e mande si we gran moun yo nan lakou'an*
*Yo poko we mwen, Yo poko we mwen*
*Terrr'a glisse la. Yo poko we mwen*

As the hurricane ravaged Okap, Ti Jocelyne sang until peace and sleep arrived.

\*\*\*

Ti Jocelyne fixated on the six dead bodies. What did the sleep of death feel like? Did the men in front of her actually disappear? Were their souls in this air conditioned room close to their bodies or were their souls following their loved ones? The small offering table normally covered with rhum bottles, drawings and bowls was replaced by a large concrete alter in the center of the north facing wall. The arched roof seemed exaggerated by the *poto mitan* which made the roof structurally and spiritually sound. Three beds against the east, three beds against the west, and the round metallic *poto mitan* centered the polished concrete altar adorned by sequined rhum bottles, dried coconut shells, calabash gourds, candles, foodstuffs and powders in numerous glass containers of various shapes and colors.

Ti Jocelyne went into the next room to grab the broom and dust pan. She swept the cold concrete floor while being careful not to sweep the broom over her feet. She moved the dust and debris away from the altar to the front door and gathered the dirt into the dustpan. With the front door opened, Ti Jocelyne tossed the dirt outside and said calmly:

"For all those I do not see."

Ti Jocelyne positioned six large glass encased white candles by each lifeless body. Out of her *djakout* bag came a bundle of cigars, packaged coffee, grilled peanuts, bread and a large swath of purple cloth. They were arranged on the altar as an offering to Baron Samedi. Ti Jocelyne unwrapped two human skulls. One represented good and the other represented evil-- the grave doesn't distinguish between the two. With the offerings on the altar, Ti Jocelyne lifted a large clear plastic bag of powder from the *djakout* hitched to her left hip. Her *vèvè* powder was a special mix of cornmeal flour, bark ashes and eggshells freshly ground in her mortar and pestle.

Talented *mambos* patiently approached the preparations and never rushed any aspect of the ceremony. The foundation of any successful spell was patience and attention to detail. Ti Jocelyne clenched a handful of the powder into her fist and carefully drew Papa Legba's *vèvè* around the base of the *poto mitan* to salute him as the intermediary between the living, the dead and unassigned spirits. Ti Jocelyne aligned a bottle of *kleren* rhum and a tall glass bottle of honey at the base of the freshly drawn *vèvè* to implore Papa Legba's spirit to join them in the room. The *vèvè* was complete, the altar was well spread, the room was clean and the dead bodies were covered in talc.

Ti Jocelyne hoisted a dried gourd of seeds and a hollowed wooden goblet while twirling before the Papa Legba *vèvè* until entranced by her chant:

*Jete d'lo nan lakou'an, aye*
*Rassemble nan lakou'an heye*
*Papa Legba kampe n'an barrieye'a, yaye*
*Papa Legba ouvrie barrieye, heye*

*Throw water into the yard, eh*
*Assemble them into the yard, hey hey*
*Papa Legba stands in the barrier, yeah*
*Papa Legba open the barrier, hey hey*

Ti Jocelyne sang until the spirit of Papa Legba entered. Another handful of powder traced Baron Samedi's *vèvè* on the base of the metal *poto mitan* support beam. The sifted powder was shaped into a large cross atop a rectangular tombstone and another rectangular box flanked by two shaped coffins. Inside each shape, she dropped powder in the form of criss crosses, asterisks, stars and plus marks until Baron Samedi's *vèvè* opened the final barrier. Ti Jocelyne sang again:

*Yo di Bawon pa lwa, aye*
*Mwen konne bawon c'est lwa l'ye*
*Yo di Bawon pa lwa, aye*
*Mwen konne bawon c'est lwa l'ye*
*Yo di Bawon pa lwa, aye*
*Mwen konne bawon c'est lwa l'ye*
*Yo di Bawon pa lwa, aye*
*Mwen konne bawon c'est lwa l'ye*

*They say Bawon isn't a spirit god, eh*
*I know Baron is a spirit god, he is*
*They say Bawon isn't a spirit god, eh*
*I know Baron is a spirit god, he is*
*They say Bawon isn't a spirit god, eh*
*I know Baron is a spirit god, he is*
*They say Bawon isn't a spirit god, eh*
*I know Baron is a spirit god, he is*

Ti Jocelyne sang the same words until she heard
no sound. Not the step of her feet, nor the shake of
the seed-filled gourds. Yet, as Gwo Pierro, had
instructed her long ago, she never sang the "take me
home, take me home" part of the chant. She didn't
need to ask why; it would invite the *lwas* to take her
home with them. Ti Jocelyne made offerings to
welcome the *lwas* into the room. She let them sit and
drink and dance by using her body as the
intermediary. She grabbed the final talc mixture and
doused the heads of the six dead bodies until there
was no more powder.

When the full heat of the sun entered; it was time to hike downhill to meet the road where the *taptap* bus would pick up passengers. Ti Jocelyne went into the back room, straightened the bed sheets and reattached the empty *djakout* bag to her hip and conducted one last inspection of the six lifeless men. Their jaws were secured with cheesecloths tied into knots above their heads. Their bodies remained as dead as could reasonably be expected.

# 10 SAMANTHA SAVIN

*Miami, Florida*

Samantha's parents were asking about her plans after graduation. She still didn't have an academic job offer. They couldn't understand why someone would go to school for so many years to become a teacher. There was no distinction between teaching at a high school and becoming a university professor. In their eyes, both were thankless low paying jobs. Her father had a conniption when she explained that newly appointed university professors are lucky to earn sixty thousand dollars a year. After all, he earned fifty-five thousand dollars a year driving taxis and he didn't even have a degree. Going to school and not getting well-paid seemed like a scam to her family.

With that in mind, and bundles of university academic post rejection letters received, Samantha applied for non-academic jobs everywhere she could. She was scheduled to receive her doctorate in the next few months and hadn't received an academic job offer anywhere. She had applied to every available microbiology assistant professor position in the United States and Canada and was only invited to five interviews: University of Ottawa, University of Nebraska-Lincoln, University of Alabama, the Eastern Kentucky University, the University at Buffalo and the University of Manitoba. Three rejections and two unanswered email chains later she felt her academic prospects completely disappear and sent résumés to pharmaceutical companies like Novartis in Switzerland, Ache in Brazil, Pfizer in New York, Divitiae Pharma in Miami, and another forty different companies.

Divitiae Pharma had a new genetic engineering department and planned to expand its microbiology laboratory. She had submitted her resume on the company website and a month later was on a plane from Charles de Gaulle Airport to Miami. Samantha would stay with her uncle and his wife. Paris was dreary and Samantha loved leaving her black turtleneck behind. At Miami International Airport, she rented the cheapest car available and drove to her uncle's house.

The next day, she put on a white linen skirt suit and pinned up her straightened hair before Miami's humidity intervened. She stuffed caramel leather pumps that perfectly matched her skin tone into a tote bag before doing one last underarm smell check.

Samantha was prepared for the interview to take the entire day but packed a towel, bathing suit, book and a pair of cut-off denim shorts in a separate bag to relax on South Beach afterwards, just in case. Samantha slipped on her flip-flops and sunglasses and hurried out the door; she threw her beach bag, leather tote and white blazer on the front passenger seat and braced herself for 95 South traffic into Miami Beach.

This was a different type of company. The parking lot was lined with hundreds of trees and colorful asphalt signs directing traffic. The building was composed of sun reflecting metal and sea green glass and the meticulous landscaping accentuated the movement of the palm trees. Samantha was impressed before she went inside. If they went to this much trouble to pick the flowers outside, their in-person interview must be intense. She put on her high heels, let down her long hair, stepped out of the car and walked over to the passenger door. Samantha put on her white linen blazer, grabbed her bag and was prepared for anything they had.

Samantha completed an extensive round of research on the people who would be interviewing her; they were world-class scientists with international peer-reviewed journal credits. Working in academia was her first choice, but she comforted herself with the fact that the private sector offered rigorous research and higher paying salaries. She entered through the large sliding double glass doors and was greeted by a blonde receptionist who invited her to sit on one of the white sofas. She was promptly served a glass of cool cucumber mint water. Whenever Samantha arrived in new places, she kept a mental count of the number of black people. Everyone who came in, out and around the lobby was white, except for one cleaning lady who looked like she was from South America.

Samantha sipped her water. A sixty something year old man, with an easy gait wearing a starched blue button down shirt, khakis and tan suede shoes made his way through the white hallway. He stopped at the receptionist's desk and was nodded in Samantha's direction. He introduced himself with an outstretched hand.

"Hello, I'm Drew Michaels. We are so happy to have you meet our team today."

Samantha promptly placed the cold glass, which she had intentionally held with her left hand, on the table and extended her dry right hand to the interviewer.

"Dr. Michaels, thank you for inviting me. I look forward to learning more about the company, and your research in particular."

As Samantha followed, a beautiful woman with long dark wavy hair entered the lobby accompanied by six tall, muscular black men dressed in expensive suits. The men carried briefcases and said nothing. The woman talked on her cell phone straight past the receptionist's desk into another corridor. Seven, Samantha thought, seven people of color in the company. Without betraying her internal thoughts, she smiled coyly at her interviewer as he made a dull joke about Miami International Airport. Samantha laughed and accompanied Drew Michaels into a large conference room.

The bright room had a round table with a large hole in its center and could easily seat two dozen employees. Three other interviewers stood to introduce themselves and shake Samantha's hand. By the time she shook the last person's hand, the job was within her reach. Samantha had a game plan: be funny, charming, tell light-hearted jokes all while referencing chemical formulas and the latest articles on microbiological research. The interviewers smiled at each other and needed one more question answered: was she familiar with CRISPR-Cas9? Their lab had received a surge of testing samples that required a series of CRISPR-cas9 tests.

"Tell us what you know about CRISPR-Cas9 research?" The male interviewer asked.

Samantha was elated. She had printed out the last three articles that the interviewers had published on CRISPR-Cas9 to read on her flight and she watched hours of their panel discussions and presentations on YouTube. Samantha's research concentrated on the cholera outbreak in Haiti, but she had a solid understanding of gene therapy and could follow the conversation on the new technology.

"Mark, I've been following your research and it's quite exciting. The CRISPR/Cas system is a prokaryotic immune system that confers resistance to foreign genetic elements such as those present within plasmids and phages that provides a form of acquired immunity. RNA harboring the spacer sequence helps Cas proteins recognize and cut exogenous DNA. Other RNA-guided Cas proteins cut foreign RNA. CRISPRs are found in approximately 40% of sequenced bacterial genomes and 90% of sequenced archaea. A simple version of the CRISPR/Cas system, CRISPR/Cas9, has been modified to edit genomes. By delivering the Cas9 nuclease complexed with a synthetic guide RNA into a cell, the cell's genome can be cut at a desired location, allowing existing genes to be removed and/or new ones added. Particularly interesting are the potential applications of CRISPR/Cas genome editing techniques such as medicine and crop seed enhancement." Samantha said while smiling confidently.

Her second interviewer, a forty-something woman with short blonde hair and brown tortoise shell glasses, wanted to make Samantha sweat.

"What faults do you see in our research?"

"I wouldn't characterize the trials and errors that create great research as faults. It would discourage the potential for further groundbreaking research, wouldn't you agree?"

Drew Michaels was impressed by her poise.

"Well then, how would you strengthen our research?"

"I wouldn't want to pretend that I have mastered your decade long research and expertise by reading some of your articles. That would be incredibly presumptuous, but if I join your team, I would concentrate on the recurring questions regarding CRISPR cas9 research in general, such as how can we control the unintended off-target consequences of gene editing? If the team creates a gene editing sequence to cure blindness in mice, then the unintended consequences must never be worse than blindness. Secondly, I know it isn't glamourous or sexy, but I would raise red flags about basic mistakes such as misidentifying genes, mislabeling genetic defects, and increasing the number of animal subjects used in the research."

"Well said." Came from the other interviewer, Dr. Stevens, "But can you tell me how you developed a sense of gene editing while the majority of your doctoral research has concentrated on the cholera outbreak in Haiti? What I mean to say, well, is you would essentially be leaving your research behind."

"I am looking for the opportunity to learn and become a more nuanced research practitioner. Even though my microbiological research assessed the causes of the 2010 cholera outbreak in Haiti, I did complete coursework on gene and DNA research and have experience collecting samples in the harshest of conditions. I also developed the ability to conduct effective community engagement and obtained patient histories and ongoing medical health assessments from 2012, 2013, 2014 and so on. I was able to cultivate international institutional support from researchers at my home institution at the Université de Paris Descartes and form new relationships at Health Canada and the University of Ottawa. And I essentially accomplished research at the highest levels without any large-scale institutional funding. I self-financed my research travel by teaching English and selling antiques at the Marché-aux-Puces on Saturdays. I know how to make a dollar out of fifteen cents and I would certainly be able to help this team.

The interviewers smiled at each other and tacitly agreed that she was it. The only remaining question was whether she would pass the company's rigorous security screening and sign the ironclad privacy and non-compete agreement.

Drew Michaels thanked Samantha as she closed her moleskin notepad and grabbed her leather bag. With a beaming smile and perfectly tailored white suit, she was the portrait of wealth and good things. Drew walked her to the reception area where she smiled.

"It was an honor meeting your team today. Thank you for taking the time to share insight on your research."

"The pleasure was all ours."

Samantha thanked the receptionist and floated to her rent-a-car. In the car, she kicked off her high heels and put on the flip-flops she had tossed onto the passenger seat.

It was 11:43 a.m. and Samantha was determined to soak up as much Florida sunshine before flying back to soggy Paris. She pulled sunglasses out of the tote bag and was ready to spend the rest of the day at the beach. Her plans were to change into her bathing suit, get a light sandwich, some oranges, a bottle of water, and read Chester Himes's *If He Hollers Let Him Go* on the beach. Samantha loved spending time alone. It centered her.

A veteran at solitary activities, she drove away from Divitiae Pharma and kept her eyes open for a local place to grab a sandwich. The traffic moved smoothly but it was hard to turn into certain restaurants. From behind a red light, a white picket fence made a restaurant shine. When the light turned green, she turned into the Miami Cafe 2000 parking lot. Univision was on the television screen, she heard the staff speaking Spanish and saw black beans and fried plantains on the plates and realized it was a Cuban restaurant. Samantha was disappointed; Cuban food was like Haitian food: heavy. The concept of light lunch did not exist. Whole wheat bread would never have entered their doors. She smiled at the waitress and flipped through the menu

"Hello, how are you. I would like Turkey and avocado on a hero with lettuce, tomatoes, salt and pepper with oil and vinegar"

The waitress came from behind the counter and asked weirdly.

"Hero?"

"Yeah, you know, the long bread for sandwiches."

The waitress was more confused, all she heard was long bed. Samantha repeated herself a couple of times and it was getting her nowhere. A tall tan man with blond hair approached the counter.

"Maria, she wants a turkey sandwich on the bread you use for the Cubano sandwiches." Chris said without missing a beat.

Samantha smiled as a nervous reflex.

"Do you have deli turkey?"

"Sorry mama, we only have chicken cutlet. Is that ok?"

Chris faced Samantha:

"Have you ever tried their Cubano sandwich?"

"No, it's my first time here."

"You have to try the Cubano. It's a must." Chris winked at Maria behind the counter and asked her to put her sandwich on his bill.

"I'm sorry but I can't accept." Samantha said while pulling out her debit card.

"Listen, you're taking a risk on the sandwich. If you don't like it then at least you didn't waste your money. Plus, free food always tastes better."

Samantha laughed and placed her card back into her bag.

"What are you drinking?

"Water."

"Maria, lemme get a large bottle of water too."

She couldn't believe this guy, he was calm, quiet and funny in an unobvious way. They were both waiting for their sandwich and Samantha got a glimpse of the TV news coverage and was shocked. Reports of mutilated bodies across Miami scared her. Without realizing it, she was talking to herself again:

"This is crazy. What the hell is this?"

Chris heard something underneath her breath.

"Trust me, it is crazy. It's been happening more."

With a deliberate flick of her wrist, Maria, who hated seeing Chris eat by himself every day, pulled out one of Cupid's arrows and placed both of their orders into the same large brown paper bag.

"Here you go Chris: two Cubano sandwiches, one malta, two bottles of water and I gave you a free fruit salad. You and your new friend, go eat together. It's bad luck to eat alone. Never eat alone."

Chris picked up the large brown bag.

"Join me for lunch?"

Chris was handsome and seemed nice enough but Samantha didn't trust anyone.

"How do I know you're not a serial killer?"

"Do I look like a serial killer?"

"They never do. It's always some regular guy from a regular neighborhood that has the chopped bodies in his basement."

Maria heard Samantha's comment and laughed out loud.

"I can promise you I'm not a serial killer."

"How could you possibly prove it?" Samantha laughed.

Chris presented his police shield and ID. Samantha read it closely and noticed a gun had been discretely lodged on the left side of his belt this entire time.

"You're a cop."

Maria interjected.

"Yes, mama. He comes in almost every day and he's a good guy."

Chris blushed.

"You ordered your sandwich for one person to go, so I'm guessing you were going to eat it at your desk alone."

"Actually no, I was going to eat my sandwich alone on the beach."

"Perfect, then you'll definitely need me. Where are you going to park your car on Ocean Drive? Come with me. You drive your car, and I'll drive my car. When we get there, I'll put my parking pass in your windshield so you can park anywhere you like. Deal? We can eat our sandwiches on the beach."

Samantha couldn't fight it, Chris was cute in a golden retriever sort of way. Affable and intrinsically non-threatening, something about him put her at ease.

"OK. I was going to the beach anyway and it's a public place."

Chris grabbed food and pinched Maria's elbow and dropped a twenty dollar tip on the counter:

"As always, thanks for everything."

Chris opened the restaurant door for Samantha.

"I'm in the truck over there, you can follow me down to the beach, I promise you everything is on the up and up. I'll even give you my food too. If you feel nervous at any time, just drive away."

"OK."

She got into her car and Chris placed the food on the backseat. Chris drove his truck straight to Ocean Drive with Samantha's car behind him. They arrived on Ocean Drive in less than ten minutes and Chris double parked his car by a space marked 'no parking at any time.' He motioned to Samantha to park her car in the empty space. As she angled into the space, Chris grabbed his official Miami Beach PD parking pass and walked to her car. When she completed the full left hand turn to straighten the car, Chris handed Samantha his parking pass.

"Leave this on your dashboard and you can park here with no problem."

Chris drove a little further up the block and parked his car in another unauthorized parking spot and placed copies of his shield, ID and parking pass on his dashboard. Samantha grabbed the large beach bag and the food on the backseat. She lowered the passenger side window and placed the car key directly underneath the driver's side car mat. No self-respecting thief would break into a Ford focus with the selection of Ferraris, Mercedes, Lamborghinis, and BMW's that regularly cruised Ocean Drive.

He jogged from the other end of the street to grab the food and beach bag from Samantha.

"What do you have in this bag? It's so heavy."

Samantha laughed and placed a smaller handbag in view.

"It's because everything can't fit into this one."

Samantha and Chris strolled up the sidewalk into a grassy patch until their feet hit the sand. She kicked off her sandals and ran her bare feet through the sand in sheer delight. The sun, the sand and the ocean breeze lowered her defenses around this new person. Samantha had a talent for adapting to different places and today was no exception. They arrived at a certain point in the sand and Samantha motioned to Chris for her bag.

"I can open up my blanket here, it's as good a spot as any."

Chris helped her smooth out the blanket. Samantha watched him untie his shoelaces, pull off his socks, and roll the hem of his pants before removing his black polo to expose his bare chest. He sat on the blanket with the sun shining in his hazel eyes.

Samantha was hesitant to wear a bathing suit in front of a guy she had just met. Yet, out of the corner of her eye, she saw two topless European women sunbathing. The women reclined unabashedly on their backs while their oiled breasts openly kissed the sunshine. Samantha felt less bashful. She reasoned with herself. No need to put on her bathing suit; instead, she would simply remove her white linen skirt and sit in her plain black panties, black bra and white camisole. She folded her skirt and sat next to Chris.

"So, where are you from?"

"I'm from Coconut Grove."

"Where's that?"

"Wait, you're not from South Florida?"

"No, I flew in yesterday for a job interview and I'm staying with my uncle and aunt."

"So where's home?"

"My family is in New York, so that's home."

"You must love New York"

"New York is OK, right now I need a job. I'm not tied to any place, I'll go wherever I get the best offer."

"What if you don't know anyone there?" Chris spoke with mouthfuls of his Cubano sandwich.

"If there is salt and there's water, I'll be fine. I'll be fine anywhere I go. I mean as long as there isn't a war or something, most places tend to be the same.

People go between work and home until they find their own rhythm."

Samantha recognized a spirit of sincerity.

"How long have you been a cop?"

"Oh, I've been on the job for fifteen no, sixteen years."

"Wow, you're a veteran."

Chris laughed and found her delightful. Every time she laughed at him, he rolled his eyes in a non-threatening way, which made Samantha laugh even more.

"Where did you interview?"

"It was a job with Divitiae Pharma"

"I've seen their commercials on TV with those warnings that the drugs might cause paralysis, seizures, or death."

Samantha laughed.

"That's all pharma companies. They are trying to avoid lawsuits."

Samantha and Chris spent the rest of the afternoon like old friends. Neither one wanted to leave. Their conversation was effortless. Samantha was surprised that Chris was so well-read. He referenced NASA articles, thoroughly understood Black Lives Matter issues, was a fan of the Young Turks, and was upset about how climate change was destroying South Florida. He even knew some Creole catch phrases. Samantha thought all cops were racist imbeciles too stupid to pass high school trigonometry.

She hadn't tasted her sandwich but was sipping from her bottle of water.

"This is crazy?"

"What?"

"I had a lot of misconceptions about you before we sat down. I work under the assumption that all cops are racist, trigger-happy, morons."

"Ugh, don't get me wrong there are plenty of those guys on the force. Trust me. I'm afraid of them too and I have a gun. Have you ever tried to talk to them? Impossible."

Samantha laughed so hard that she snorted like a baby pig. She couldn't stop laughing. Samantha's laughter became infectious and Chris laughed uncontrollably too.

"Are you on Instagram?"

"I am."

Chris opened his Instagram account and showed her the screen.

"What's your handle?"

"It's just my name, Samantha Savin."

# 11 GWO PIERRO

*Okap, Haiti*

The horizon was a blend of purple, pink, and orange as Gwo Pierro prepared another fabulous party at Labadee Beach. The cruise ships and tourist hordes were long gone and headed to their next island destination. Their departure meant the beach would be reopened to locals. Gwo Pierro had a long standing arrangement with one of the cruise ship staffers for private use of the area.

Gwo Pierro welcomed his rich guests with self-effacing humility. He was generous and made people feel better about themselves when they entered his sphere. Times had changed considerably from when he first returned to Haiti from Paris in the 1970's. Gwo Pierro had a silent way of influencing people. He was gay but nobody ever asked or seemed to be bothered by it.

The beach was decorated with tall hurricane oil lamps and elevated cocktail tables anchored into the sand. The DJ table was mounted on an elevated brick floor adjacent to a table of shrimp hors d'oeuvres, spicy chicken skewers and an endless array of mouthwatering morsels. To the side, another long table was covered with three enormous glass canisters each filled with different flavors of punch being ladled into ice filled glasses by three gorgeous chocolate complexioned barmaids wearing large afros and identical white halter top dresses. Their shoulders and collarbones glimmered with bronze powder. They were distinguishable by one trait: the woman who ladled the neon pink punch wore a bright neon pink lipstick and neon pink afro wig, the woman who poured the orange punch wore a bright neon orange lipstick and neon orange wig the woman who poured the purple punch wore a similarly bright purple neon lipstick and wig. Gwo Pierro was meticulous, he planned every detail and the lipstick color worn by staff was no exception.

By the time the sun set, Gwo Pierro had over one hundred guests on the enclosed beach promenade. The food, the drinks, and the DJ were a level above the brick covered promenade, while the dance floor was located down three steps and directly on the sand. Breaking the monotony of high-end pomp and circumstance was the key to any successful party.

He flicked off his shoes and asked one of his guests, an eighty-year old widowed mother, to dance. As they descended the three steps, Gwo Pierro smiled and whispered something in her ear. He gently removed her strappy heels and led her to the middle of the sand to dance. The DJ was in sync with the crowd and dropped the first bass beat to Carimi's *Bò Kote w* guaranteeing a secondary delay until the other guests joined. Gwo Pierro danced with the old lady like she was a *demoiselle* at her first dance. She was instantly at ease with him, grew giddy, and enjoyed that night in a way she hadn't enjoyed in years. By the next song, the majority of the guests were dancing with abandon.

Gwo Pierro excused himself to nibble some spicy shrimp from one of the platters and then another. He was about to stuff a third piece of shrimp in his mouth, when a middle-aged gentleman tapped him on the shoulder.

"Don't tell me." Gwo Pierro yelled, "It can't be. Give me the date of the last time I saw you. It's not the same young doctor Richard Savin who had to escape from Baby Doc in the middle of the night, that's looking at me in my face right now?"

"*Apa*, you haven't forgotten me."

"I remember you and the other new doctors tried to mobilize young people after Baby Doc came to power. You thought because he was only nineteen, fat and stupid that you could remove him. You had a case of democracy follies." Gwo Pierro said through an infectious laugh.

"Nothing even changed after Baby Doc left the country." Richard sighed.

"True power rests in the hands of those behind the leader. When the father died, it meant that Papa Doc supporters had to double down to protect his useless son in order to safeguard their own interests." Gwo Pierro sipped the purple punch. "Richard, you have to introduce me to this beautiful woman you brought here with you this evening."

"Oh excuse me. This is my wife, Eloise."

"How did you manage to find such a beauty?"

"Her cousin was dating Manno, you remember him, don't you? We met when I went to their house for a communion."

"There is a name, I haven't heard in years. I do remember Manno. Funny, sharp, soccer player, he could kick the ball and idiots would hit their heads on the goal posts trying to defend the shots."

Everyone within earshot laughed. Gwo Pierro motioned to a server to bring another round of punch.

"What a miracle you're back in Haiti."

"My wife and I come every August for two weeks to provide free clinical health services in different small towns. We are the only doctors some patients will see the entire year."

The DJ started playing Digital Express and Richard and his wife joined the other guests by dancing barefoot in the sand. Gwo Pierro saw one of his guests standing unaccompanied and said:

"Let's join them, shall we?"

They danced until Gwo Pierro needed another drink. While sipping another helping of punch a young man, no older than nineteen, wearing dirty ripped clothes forced himself past the security team insisting that he had to speak to Gwo Pierro. His father had sent him with a message and it was absolutely urgent. The head guard led him into the fête by the arm.

"What's going on here?" Gwo Pierro asked.

"Boss, my father sent me to warn you. I came here straightaway on my neighbor's motorbike." The young man said through hurried breaths.

"Then what is it?"

"My father… is Jean-Georges, he works for Alex Duperville and… he is sending men to kill you tonight. The men are already on their way."

Gwo Pierro searched his mind, Alex Duperville, Alex Duperville, he found it. The vetiver oil exporter whose vapid cousin Gwo Pierro had dispersed of long ago. It was time to summon help. These weren't evil spirits coming for him, but armed men being paid to kill.

Always ready, Gwo Pierro's trucks were perpetually stocked with machine guns and rifles. People assumed the men driving the trucks were chauffeurs; this was a job where he didn't hire women. The spirit of jealousy was more dangerous than any *lwa* he had ever encountered. There were plenty of spells to defeat evil spirits, but the only way to deal with street thugs was to fight them as a street thug yourself. Gwo Pierro found his head of security and told him to assemble the other men in front of the main entrance gate. Gwo Pierro had earned the respect of his security detail over the years and tonight they would have to work as a team.

Gwo Pierro passed through the front gate towards the group of twelve assembled men. He went to the trunk of the first SUV and grabbed the AK-47. Even though no one had ever seen him sell cocaine, the war chest of guns that Gwo Pierro stored in the SUV trunks embellished his reputation as a notorious cartel affiliate. His security drivers had assumed Gwo Pierro was a drug dealer and that created a special brand of invincibility. Gwo Pierro's true strength was not invincibility but his uncanny ability to remain level headed. Gwo Pierro mounted the side of the SUV and held onto the hood of the truck with one hand and waved the AK -47 with the other.

"Listen, the children of those who are no good are coming here. When they arrive they won't ask your name. They won't care if you're a driver. They won't ask if you have a wife or children at home. The enemy comes to steal, kill and destroy everything you hold dear. And, I'll tell you another thing. They won't hesitate to kill you on sight. Strap on your manhood because they are coming. We'll show them that there are no games being played here. In the same motion, Gwo Pierro drummed on the top of the SUV:

"*Bay yo. Bay yo. Bay yo. Bay yo.*"

"Give it to them. Give it to them. Give it to them."

The men banged on the car hoods and screamed at the top of their lungs:

"*Bay yo, Bay yo, Bay yo.*"

Gwo Pierro grabbed his head of security.

"How many more guns do we have in the trucks?"

"Boss, we have at least three dozen more... each car always has at least three to five guns in the back at any moment."

"Good, I'll go find more men."

He returned to the party where his guests were still enjoying themselves. He went straight for the DJ and grabbed the microphone. The DJ immediately turned down the music.

Most of his guests had guns in their cars and homes. Like his compatriots, they had learned to shoot by hunting squabs and pigeons as children. Now as adults, his male counterparts kept guns because robbers shot people in their homes with no fear of police or law or order. Family members of the deceased were often forced to seek their own justice. Gwo Pierro figured that Alex Duperville wanted to kill him because he had taken the life of his cousin years ago.

"My friends, there is no other way to say it. I have received word that *vakabons*, well-armed v*akabons,* are on their way here to kill us. You know just as well as I do, that when they arrive they will ravage us all. A dozen men are outside the gate with guns but I am not sure that they'll be able to stop those who are coming. We have more guns, what I need to know is whether anyone here will stand with us. It's dark and there is only one road that leads out of here. There is nowhere to hide on the beach, we are exposed. Even if I find a helicopter pilot to leave his house right now, only four of us will fit and he still might not get here in time. What I need to ask you right now is whether or not you will fight?"

Yves, an old school friend, was the first to stand.

"We can't let them kill us."

Gwo Pierro scanned the rest of the crowd

"This is not the moment to be interesting. This is a moment of testicular fortitude."

A large group of men stepped up to the DJ booth.

"Good."

Gwo Pierro went to the edge of the short staircase and grabbed his shoes. He sat down on one of the benches, dusted the sand off his feet and buckled the straps on his leather sandals. They weren't ideal for fighting, but they were certainly better than trying to run barefoot on gravel. The other men followed his lead and put on their shoes. The waitresses cried and pulled tablecloths off the tables and huddled together in a dark corner on the beach. A cohort of old ladies prayed to the invisibles.

He escorted the partygoers to the front gate to meet his security detail and gave guns to whoever would take them. Richard's wife grabbed a semi-automatic and placed it in between her legs so she could braid her hair.

A faint burning smell covered them. It was slowly replaced with an unidentifiable pungency. It took a minute, but Gwo Pierro pinpointed the smell by closing his eyes. And it hit him at once: the scent of burning talc. Weak at first, it grew so strong that guests far from the front gate had to breathe through their shirts. Some used the sharp carving knives from the buffet table to cut pieces from the table cloths and tied them around the lower part of their faces and noses.

Several rounds of gunshots were unleashed. Gwo Pierro ran to the front gate and his men joined him. He cocked his automatic gun at a dozen brightly painted *taptap* buses herding hundreds of bare chested zombies completely covered in a mixture of talcum powder and soot. They swayed without making any large movements. Gwo Pierro's courageous guards were struck by a debilitating bout of fear.

The zombies had been able bodied young men. Their muscles ripped through the layers of talcum powder doused over them. The soulless men wore no clothes, except for one piece of white fabric wrapped around their loins. The conversion had recently occurred. Their faces had no stubble and their bodies showed no signs of physical wear or tear.

Gwo Pierro had never seen such a thing. Each zombie held a piece of bloody raw meat in their hands. Everyone knew not to feed zombies salt because it would interfere with the zombie powder. But he had never thought about what would happen if the zombies ate meat. Hardworking men in Haiti could work day in and day out and still go more than a month without meat ever touching their plates. It had never occurred to Gwo Pierro that feeding zombies meat was a possibility. As he remained internally baffled by the idea of zombies eating meat, he saw Alex Duperville standing in the back corner of the mob.

Alex Duperville, a tall and handsome man, was a few years younger than Gwo Pierro. Wearing blue jeans, a simple black t-shirt and hiking boots, nothing about him revealed that he was a *bòkò* . Gwo Pierro thought he was experienced in zombification but he had never imagined creating zombies on such a scale.

Alex Duperville was here to settle an old family score. Gwo Pierro devoured Duperville's cousin's body through regular gifts of cocaine. It was gradual at first, the cocaine was lightly cut with the zombie powder but with each subsequent dose, Gwo Pierro mixed in more zombie powder until the presence of cocaine was nearly undetectable. As with the other lost souls, Gwo Pierro used zombie powder to get blow jobs and asshole licks from men who denied being gay. As their zombie creator, they could only hear his voice, their internal voice disappeared. His orders replaced their will. Completely transformed into soulless bodies, Gwo Pierro sold them to the highest bidder, like Alex Duperville's cousin more than twenty years ago.

Gwo Pierro, his guards and guests remained on a dangerous, yet silent level of attention, unaware of how the zombies would react. Alex Duperville raised a hand and the zombies lifted their heads like well trained dogs. He shouted calmly at the top of his voice:

*"Mangez, mangez, mwen di nou, mangez."*
"Eat, eat, I tell you, eat."

In one swift motion, the zombies forced the bloody meat to their mouths and tore through the flesh with their teeth. The taste of the blood revived an animalistic instinct tempered down millennia ago. They immediately pounced at Gwo Pierro, the guards and everyone else who dared to stand before them. The talc zombies at the front of the pack grabbed one security guard and chomped at his jugular like wolves killing their prey. The zombies pushed over each other to bite through the security guard's neck until the head teetered back-and-forth on a hinge of flesh. Blood spouted everywhere and lured more soulless bodies to feed on the living before them.

Gwo Pierro reassessed his position. The vicious shredding of the security guard destroyed assumptions about systematically shooting to defend the location. Everyone instantly scattered in thirty different directions and were so afraid that they couldn't hold the guns, let alone shoot straight.

One guard tried shooting them in the head. It didn't work. The zombies advanced through bullets blowing whole chunks off their skulls to the ground. Pop, pop, pop, pop. They shot endless rounds and emptied magazine clips. The zombies pursued their trajectories like chickens running with their heads cut off. Simon, Gwo Pierro's most loyal guard, grabbed his CV Scorpion and underestimated its recoil strength with the preliminary shots fired. The firearm lacked a stock and at least a dozen bullets went into the air. With the hundreds of zombies quickly approaching, Simon tried again but the gun was jammed. The lever refused to work.

Another guard was so scared that he climbed a sloped palm tree. As Simon struggled with the gun, one zombie and then the next and then a third climbed the tree yearning for a piece of blood filled flesh. A zombie grabbed his leg and took a solid bite of his left calf tossing him to the ground. Another instinctively bit the side of his face and the side of his neck gushed blood. The smell of fresh blood attracted more zombies closer to the gate.

Alex Duperville stood far away but close enough to observe the carnage. Gwo Pierro anchored his leg to the lower gate grill and leveraged his arm on its forged iron design. Shots fired from the corner like a sniper cleared holes through zombie chests. Bullets splattered chunks from dead torsos. Zombies staggered to their fall. The loss of blood dropped the undead to a final death.

Guests followed Gwo Pierro's example and blew holes into the chests of the zombies as they approached the gate. Richard yelled at Gwo Pierro in the middle of the mayhem:

"Did you know he was burning magic?"

Gwo Pierro hunched lower and placed more of his weight on the forged iron gate.

"Listen, no one ever knows what anyone else is doing."

More zombies came close and Richard shot the right half of one chest off. Incessant gunshots and screams filled the air. Blood spewed uncontrollably from the growing number of bullet pierced bodies. Blood flew out the undead as other talc covered bodies dropped to the soil.

Richard's wife, Eloise, was on the ground with the gun perched on the edge of a large boulder. She held a steady head and hand while men ran about in fear screaming:

"*Amvey!, Amvey!, Amvey!*"

Eloise shot rounds through the chests of oncoming zombies until they bled and collapsed. The flesh seeking zombies coveted the taste of bloody flesh still on their lips. Eloise had maintained aloof conversations in French the entire night, but under duress only Creole existed:

"Vize lestomak yo. Vize lestomak yo. Vize lestomak yo."

"Shoot them in the chest. Shoot them in the chest. Shoot them in the chest."

Gwo Pierro heard Eloise shouting, so he shouted too:

"Shoot them in the chest. Shoot them in the chest."

A nearby security guard and another party guest, then the next guard and the following guest repeated the same refrain until the guns fired out in complete unison. Pop, pop, pop, pop, pop, pop, pop. The gunshots flew back and forth until they reached a rhythmic marching band crescendo. The remaining members of Gwo Pierro's security detail and the other survivors rallied the remaining rounds of ammunition to shoot through the chests of the zombies until the soulless figures bled to their end.

Duperville saw his army of zombies decimated to a simple platoon. He escaped to his truck and instructed his driver to flee.

Gwo Pierro couldn't believe that Alex Duperville and his men were giving up so quickly. Did they come all this way, just to leave? Duperville had carried out his plan with military level precision and caused a major panic but pulled away before the full damage was achieved. What did Duperville want? If he wanted him dead, it would have been easier to show up at his home and kill him while he slept. Gwo

Pierro didn't keep any security at his house and he walked the streets without guards. This was not a case of revenge.

Some of his guards and guests had deserted. Gwo Pierro didn't hold it against them. Fear paralyzes people. Adrenaline fueled flight response is real. He needed to calm everyone down. Gwo Pierro stopped shooting and called out to everyone and stomped his right foot like a slow bass drum. And in the midst of the chaos, Gwo Pierro began a slow steady chant:

*Yo dit bawon pa lwa'l ye*
*Yo dit bawon pa lwa'l ye*
*Gade'm konne c'est lwa'l ye*
*Yo dit bawon pa law'l ye*
*Mene yo alle tonnere*

*They say baron isn't a spirit*
*They say baron isn't a spirit*
*Look at my understanding of his spirit*
*They say baron isn't a spirit*
*Take them away, thunder*

It was a familiar chant even to those who had never cast a spell, or those who went to Adventiste church on Saturdays. They all knew the words and chanted along. One after another, each guard, each guest sang the words like a familiar nursery rhyme discarded during adolescence. As they sang, a trancelike calm replaced their fears. A new clarity of mind to shoot straight. Pop. Pop. Pop. Rang in different directions. Through the chest, out the gut and by the kidneys--- anything to make the most amount of blood fall in the least amount of time. As the blood spurted out of the soulless men their ability to walk and bite slowed with each drop of blood released by the rapid succession of bullets.

The chanting evolved into a steady hum that Gwo Pierro's people used to remain steadfast while confronting their childhood nightmares. Tack. Tack. Tack. More bullets flew. The steady hum created a soft momentum to counter the violent haphazardness unleashed before them. Within an hour, Gwo Pierro, his guards and guests steadily hummed then shot, hummed and shed soulless blood until they had spilled the blood of the last standing zombie.

Bloodied lifeless talc bodies were everywhere. The stillness in the air testified to their collective unspeakable state of shock. When they tried to speak only rudimentary stutters left their mouths. The remaining shooters staggered in a drunken-like stupor.

It was seemingly over. Gwo Pierro was scared even after all the zombies had been bled dead. Until now, most assumed he was an affable drug dealer. Alex Duperville attacking him in such a public manner meant that Gwo Pierro's true business dealings were exposed. Gwo Pierro's mind raced back and forth. What could Alex Duperville want? He already had money. He had mastered the mysteries of the invisibles to create his own zombies.

Gwo Pierro had seen this before. Anytime Haitian people became too big and too rich, they would inevitably want one thing: to become president of Haiti. Every successful Haitian person had presidential aspirations. It was an undiagnosed sickness. Sweet Mickey and Wyclef were casualties of this generally accepted phenomenon. Everyone thought the presidency meant ultimate power and mistakenly assumed if they were president they could solve Haiti's problems. They failed to realize that power, like water, can only be held temporarily; the harder it is clasped, the easier it escapes. Gwo Pierro shunned politics. The truest form of power was hidden in the forgotten laps of poor women.

Gwo Pierro needed an army to go to war. Unleashing hundreds of zombies in public was not to be borne. He broke the only cardinal rule of Vodou: never betray the mysteries. Even Duvalier, at the height of his unbridled ruthlessness alluded to his Vodou practice through symbols, carnival folk songs, clothing, and carefully balanced Vodou propaganda to avoid causing outright hysteria. Duvalier preferred to send his police to shoot people in broad daylight so there could be no doubt in his power. His Vodou practice was intentionally elusive to safeguard popular allegiance to collective mysteries. Haiti could not stand, let alone survive, if the power that Vodou holds over her people was compromised. Alex Duperville had not only threatened Gwo Pierro but had unraveled the complicated tapestry of Vodou, politics, and poverty that sustained Haiti. Alex Duperville's days among the living were few.

Within half an hour of Gwo Pierro's calls, two helicopters and two dozen bulletproof SUV's arrived at Labadee. One driver grabbed at least twenty shovels from the back of one of the trucks. Gwo Pierro sent those with substantial injuries in the helicopters to Hôpital Universitaire Justinien. The remaining guests were safely shuttled back to Okap. The hardest part of that night would be containing the story in order to shield his next move. There was no hiding what had happened. He sent each group of guests into a different armed car and apologized profusely as he kissed them goodbye. The bodies of his deceased security guards and guests were driven to Okap to receive proper burials.

When the guests were gone, Gwo Pierro instructed the head guard to have the remaining men dig a massive grave to bury the soulless bodies. The men dug slowly. The men would need the rest of the night to dig a grave large enough to hold the countless bodies. Gwo Pierro rambled on his cell phone to organize a response. His men lowered their arms in fatigue and sheer disbelief. None of them could have imagined they would ever be so close to slaughtered zombies. It was inconceivable.

Gwo Pierro removed his torn bloody white linen shirt and stood defiantly with his bare rotund stomach; he grabbed a shovel and vigorously threw mounds of dirt to the side. The men were encouraged by the sight of their boss digging alongside them and found a reserve of force to plough through the night. The men were exhausted; yet, no one was too tired to ensure that dead remained dead. By the time the last dead body was dropped into the deep long trench, the sun hinted its intentions. Gwo Pierro sent a guard to fetch kerosene lamps left burning on the beach. The men hurled dozens of kerosene lamps into the massive grave as Gwo Pierro grabbed a bottle of rhum from one of his guards and chanted:

*Yo dit bawon pa lwa'l ye*
*Yo dit bawon pa lwa'l ye*
*Gade'm konne c'est lwa'l ye*
*Yo dit bawon pa law'l ye*
*Mene yo alle tonnere*

*They say baron isn't a spirit*
*They say baron isn't a spirit*
*Look at my understanding of his spirit*
*They say baron isn't a spirit*
*Take them away, thunder*

His guards joined the hymn until their voices reached a boisterous pitch. Gwo Pierro tossed a lighter into the trench. And the massive zombie grave blaze rivaled the early morning sun.

# 12 CHRIS

*Miami, Florida*

Chris scrolled through his social media feed and saw one of those annoying inspirational posts that women liked to share ad nauseam:

"When you lose a loved one, you'll search for them in every person you meet."

The meme made Chris uncomfortable. Samantha reminded him of the Haitian girl he loved in high school. He was a coward. At sixteen, seventeen, he had loved her but simply didn't have the courage to be with a black girl. Or had his high school crush prepared him for Samantha? Was it destiny, fulfillment of unrequited love, learning, growth or an incoherent combination of all of those things? The relationships he formed during his childhood, adolescence, failed college years and first job assignments, they had shaped him into someone. Who, exactly, Chris did not know. He was willing to think about such things when nestled in bed alongside Samantha.

It was nearly 6 o'clock on a beautiful Sunday morning and he should head outside for a run while Samantha was still in bed. He admired her svelte curvaceous frame through the sheer white sheet. He loved her. He was sure of it. He had never felt a fear like this before. He wanted her there all of the time. When she wasn't with him he worried. She was smart, beautiful, bossy and left him wanting more. She fought to get her way, which was alright because she sought the best for everyone. Chris was whole with her. It didn't matter if they were having microwave popcorn in front of the TV or at one of her boring work events. He didn't deserve her but he had to make her his own. She moved to Miami four months ago and they were together almost every day. He was complete. He was going to ask her to marry him, he was certain of it. He didn't want to scare her off by being desperate.

He loved the way her thick curls gathered into the bright purple hair net and how she wore long sexy tank tops to bed with no underwear. Chris crawled underneath the sheet and spooned his hip behind her and while placing his hand on her breast. He squeezed her tightly with his eyes wide open. It wasn't a dream. Samantha carried the faint smell of coconut oil. She slathered herself with coconut oil after her nighttime shower and her scent lingered in his sheets long after she had gone. She even stored a small glass jar of coconut oil in the nightstand for back massages which ended being applied on his shaft through a circular hand motion.

As Chris gently tugged her left nipple, Samantha found his hard dick pushing its way down the curve of her back. Samantha gyrated her hips and he moved passionately against her. Chris turned his arm around and grabbed a handful of congealed coconut oil out of the jar. He rubbed the solid oil up and down his shaft until it melted into a smooth lubricant. He returned to Samantha and was firmly enveloped in her wet warmth. She shifted onto her stomach and arched her back to feel his fullness inside her. The world of her wonderful warmth was home. He loved her bronzed skin and the fullness of her hips as they hit his balls back and forth. Watching his dick go in and out of her strengthened his erection. He leaned forward to bite her shoulder. Samantha instinctively tilted back for Chris to grab her breasts until she released out a couple of heavy sighs. Chris loved how she intuited his next move. When they made love, neither of one of them had to really speak or say more than a word or two.

"Harder." Samantha whispered.

Chris thrusted the full weight of his manhood into her until Samantha licked her fingers to rub her clitoris. They fulfilled each other's needs and climaxed together. He could never tell if he let her come first or if she was holding back her orgasm for him. It was perfect.

He loved when Samantha let her guard down. She seemed tense and on edge. She rarely relaxed. She had to-do-lists for the office, to-do-lists for her apartment, to-do-lists for her workout goals, to-do-lists for her groceries and to-do-lists to organize her to-do-lists. It was entirely too much work. She loved him and still held back parts of herself. Chris could not understand why she was always trying to prove herself. It was easier to get through to Samantha emotionally after sex but before her to-do-list took over. Chris was happy to have her with him early in the morning and late at night; her sense of purpose gave him direction.

"I love to see you like this."

"Like what?"

"Calm, relaxed, at peace."

"You're a calm person" Samantha quickly replied.

"No I'm not."

"You're like a human tranquilizer. No one can actually be upset when they're with you."

"That's not true, I get upset all the time."

"Well, it never shows."

"I feel calmer when I'm with you."

"I know, right?"

"It feels like I've known you forever"

"It does."

"What are your parents like?"

"What are your parents like?" Samantha retorted.

"Who, my parents are boring. I told you already. Nothing special. They went to college. Got married and had three kids. Now they have an empty nest and are waiting for grandkids."

"Do your parents get along?" Samantha wondered out loud.

"Yeah."

"Do they yell at each other?"

"My mother doesn't yell. She does worse-- she sends constant reminders until your ears fall off and my father is always at work."

"Well that sounds nice."

"What does that mean? That sounds nice."

"I didn't grow up like that."

"Then how did you grow up?"

"From the outside, I had two parents, three outgoing kids. But there was extreme violence in my house growing up. My father would beat my mother half the time and then gamble his whole check leaving us hungry. Most of the time, my mother was in and out of the hospital, and housing court trying to keep a roof over our heads"

"Oh, I didn't know."

"I know, no one ever knows. And no one can ever tell."

Chris felt horrible for taking his boring home life for granted. He loved Samantha even more and wanted to fill her broken spaces.

"Why did your mother stay?"

"I have no idea."

"Did your father drink?"

"Actually, no. He could barely finish a whole can of beer. Gambling was his drug of choice. And of course, the women. He was a philanderer. All over the place."

"What?"

"My father has extramarital kids, with a couple of different women."

"Ugh! Why do you think he acts like that?"

"It's the way he was reared. He thinks he's better than everyone else and didn't need to work for anything because he was born into the right family. That and he had the luck and protection of the *lwas* to keep him safe." Samantha sighed.

"Luh wah?"

"*Lwas* are like Vodou spirits, like mini Gods."

"Can I ask you a question?" Chris muttered.

"Ok."

"You practice Vodou?"

"What?" Samantha sat into an upright position.

"I mean, is it real?" Chris wondered out loud.

"Is what real?" Samantha retorted.

Samantha sat up and a long black pendant dangled between her flawless caramel breasts.

"The spells, the magic, all of it?"

"Are people in Haiti casting Vodou spells? Yes."

"Do you believe in it?"

"Do I believe that Vodou exists?"

"Does Vodou exist?"

"Yes. It exists. If you believe in anything, it has power and control over you. Like horoscopes or knocking on wood. It is real to them. They put their energy into a belief system and those beliefs have power over their lives."

"Does it have power over you?"

"But if you ask the majority of Haitians if they practice Vodou they will tell you no. By default, Vodou is a mystery where all of the secrets are never given to any of its practitioners. The *lwas*, these spirits reveal things to their practitioners at different times according to their faithfulness. Going up to a Haitian person and asking them do they practice Vodou is like asking them what kind of underwear they are wearing. It's such a private personal question, that most will never tell you the truth."

"But do you or don't you?"

"Absolutely not."

"How can I tell if you're telling the truth or if you're being private and discrete?"

"Well, most Haitian people who grow up outside of Haiti, you know in New York, Boston, Montreal, Paris and other places with lots of Haitian immigrants, are uprooted from the true cultural practice. If a Haitian person grew up outside of Haiti, they won't usually practice, and the small percentage of new wave, afro-centric Haitians who do practice Vodou aren't modest or discrete. They walk around with *lwa*s t-shirts, introduce themselves as *mambos* and *houngans* to drive business to their websites. Their Vodou practice is beyond extra."

"What does that even mean?"

"So, when a *vodwisan* serves a *lwa*, part of their practice requires them to prepare various offerings."

"And?"

"I've been to a lot of different Haitian people's houses. Old and young. Fresh off the boat and long established. Rich and poor Haitians. Light skin and dark skin. From Port-au-Prince and from the lost corners of Haiti. And I have never seen a Vodou altar just out in the open for company to see. Meanwhile, overzealous Haitian-American kids have altars and offerings out like decoration for any person who comes into their house to see and talk about their Vodou practice with everybody like a new phone or flat screen TV.

"C-c-can you cast spells?"

"Asking a random Haitian person if they can cast Vodou spells is like asking a random French person if they can bake a baguette. Baguettes are all over France, but only bakers actually prepare bread for everyone else. Well, it's the same way with Vodou, most of the Haitian people who practice don't know how to cast spells and would actually go to a *houngan* or *mambo* for that."

"So if you needed something, you would go to a *mambo* for him to cast a spell?'

"A *mambo* is a woman. A *houngan* is a man. But never, I mean never."

"How can you be so sure?"

"Listen, being initiated into Vodou and serving the *lwas* is like being in with the mob. Your house burns down, fuck you pay me. Your husband leaves you, fuck you pay me. You get sick, fuck you pay me. In Haiti, right now, a lot of them are walking around in rags with no food to feed their own children but somehow they have enough to make sure that *Erzulie* has plenty of perfume, champagne and cake. Fuck that!"

"Why does it make you so upset?"

"When we were kids, how many times did my father ever go to the supermarket and buy cupcakes and treats for us? Pretty much never. But when it came time for *mangé marassa* offerings he went all out buying cupcakes, fruit, candy, flavored colas, and every other imaginable thing that kids would like. It's complete and utter bullshit. Feeding these spirits while your own kids are going hungry. Fuck them."

"Everyone's family has issues. Don't worry about it."

Chris hit a nerve and needed to change the subject. He turned on the TV and went to the bathroom with the door open. He could see

Samantha on the bed as he peed with one eye on the toilet. He gave his dick a firm shake and returned to bed where Samantha was sitting against the headboard with her unbridled nipples. She was flipping through the channels and Chris placed his head in her lap. He loved the feel of her. She was upset and reached deep into his soul.

"I love being with you. When we are together, there is no other place I want to be." Chris lifted his head and muted the television.

"I know we only met about six months ago, and that we started dating when you moved to Miami, a little after that. But for me, Miami, even though it is home, was an empty place before you came." Chris sat up straight to hold Samantha's hand.

"This is sudden, and we haven't even discussed it, but would you marry me. You're the only one for me. You make me happy. When I thought my life was nothing, you came and completely changed my outlook. I want to make you happy, if you'll let me. Samantha will you marry me?"

Chris couldn't read her facial expressions. Chris clasped both of his hands over her hands and Samantha cried.

"Will you marry me?' Chris repeated.

"Yes. Yes." Samantha said through gentle tears.

The salt from her tears met his lips. He lowered his head to her nipple before kissing her stomach and licking her navel. Chris tasted Samantha's essence as his tongue met her clitoris. He teased the opening of her passageway with the tip of his member.

"I want you inside of me."

Chris loved Samantha sweetly. Her teeth clenched his shoulder as they grinded in a clockwise unison leading to their release.

As they snuggled underneath the sheets, Samantha nudged Chris.

"Chris, look."

"I know you're beautiful already." Chris said with his eyes closed.

"No, I mean the TV. Turn up the volume."

Chris searched the sheets, the side table and eventually found the remote control under the corner of the bed. He pressed mute and the reporter narrated:

"We are observing the situation closely and will continue to provide live updates as we receive additional information."

The television screen displayed images of the Miami swat team and dozens of ambulances parked directly outside of Divitiae Pharma.

"That's my job." Samantha got off the bed and searched for her bra. "That's my company. What the hell happened?"

Samantha went into the bathroom while speaking to Chris.

"I can't believe it. I need to know what happened. I'm going to try calling some of my co-workers to find out what happened."

Chris's phone rang and it was Rodriguez. There were multiple missed texts:

"Chris, call me back."

"Yo, Chris this is serious. I would never bother you on a Sunday morning if it wasn't serious."

"Call me back."

"Sclafani and the guys are down here. Call me back."

"Get your fingers off your dick and call me the fuck back."

Chris dialed Rodriguez.

"What's up?"

"Chris, it's bad man. Some of our guys had to put down over two dozen men today. It's the same shit. They were attacking people and biting off their faces and necks right in the middle of the day. They went into the street and the surrounding areas next to the pharma company and just started attacking people. I wasn't here but the first two cops had the side of their necks chewed off. Dead bodies on the ground, some guards, some random people and God knows who else, just dead. It's a fucking bloody mess. Get down here."

"I'm on my way."

Chris put on his jeans and searched for the black long sleeve waffle shirt he was wearing the night before. He reached for the balled socks that he had stuffed into his black duty boots. He buckled a black holster of gear around his waist. He scoured through a drawer for his dog tag and clipped his shield to the chain before knocking on the bathroom door.

"Sam. It was Rodriguez and he needs me at the crime scene."

Samantha opened the door and tucked the front tip of her loose white tank top into her tight white jeans.

"I called three of my co-workers and no one answered their phone."

Chris kissed her tenderly.

"I gotta go. I'll drop you off at home."

"No you're not. I'm coming with you."

"The site is completely closed off."

"I'm coming with you."

"Listen, you don't understand. When something bad happens, cops close ranks. Rodriguez said the cops were forced to shoot over two dozen people who worked at your company. If I had to guess, the Governor of Florida is watching this on the news right now and heads are going to roll. When a cop kills one person, whether he was right or wrong, everything gets shut down. And we all have to follow every single rule to the T. I don't even want to know what's gonna happen with so many dead bodies at one scene."

"Bring me along. Tell them I work at the company, trust me, I have my work ID, tell them I'm your first background witness." Samantha said confidently.

Chris hunched his shoulders. She was right, they needed to learn about the structure of the company and the building as quickly as possible. She was, at this point, the best person to have at his side.

# 13 TI JOCELYNE

*Okap, Haiti*

The midday sun bent gracefully into early evening. Ti Jocelyne had gone to market for groceries and returned with more than her mind could hold. Every week, she bought groceries for Didoune to prepare while babysitting her daughter during weekend work assignments. Eyes followed Ti Jocelyne through the market. It was Jean, David's son. He also worked for Gwo Pierro in the mountains. The secretive nature of their work tied them together without a word being spoken. Despite her flawless figure, Ti Jocelyne hid her increased financial position under shabby clothes. In contrast, Woody sported a different official Messi FC Barcelona jersey every day.

As Ti Jocelyne stepped away from the market, the same eyes accompanied her through the bustle of people in alleyways and side streets making their way to some urgent location. She felt the eyes on her, watching her. Street merchants balanced upright bundles of cold soda and bags of plantain chips on their heads, men pushed wheelbarrows of sugar cane on the side of the road while stray dogs searched for something to pass through their mouths. She continued among the crowds pretending to be unbothered.

An unknown male voice called out her name; she knew better than to turn around. An evil spirit could be calling towards a nefarious end; she walked unfazed and ignored the sound of her own name being called behind her. Heavy hurried foot stomps tried to catch her. Ti Jocelyne fixed her face straight ahead and adjusted her pace. The rhythm in her step pulsed after a hand clenched the side of her waist.

"I've succeeded in seeing you again."

"Where do I know you from? I'm sure we've never been introduced."

She was oblivious to young men. Building a legacy for her daughter occupied her heart. Having seen him briefly in Gwo Pierro's service and now meshed in with carnival crowds meant absolutely nothing to Ti Jocelyne.

"You don't need to pretend to be more interesting than you are... and posture as if we've never met before." Woody replied.

"I don't know you. I don't even know your name."

The strongest lies are based in truth. Ti Jocelyne honestly didn't know his name nor would she have dared asked Gwo Pierro about him.

"You know my name?"

"They call you Ti Jocelyne, the vendors, the neighbors, people at church, Gwo Pierro and everyone."

"Eh hegh, you've been meddling in my affairs."

"Your affairs? We have the same affairs. We've been working together for years and you didn't even realize it. You leave the bodies on Saturday. What do you think happens to them?"

"That doesn't concern me. You shouldn't put his business out into the street. Who sent you to talk about Gwo Pierro's affairs in front of people?" Ti Jocelyne huffed.

Ti Jocelyne seethed with anger as she secured the grocery bag with an extra knot. Her scowl made it clear that she intended on going home alone. Woody gazed at Ti Jocelyne's hips as the distance camouflaged her rage. A wave of heat seized her. She never asked Gwo Pierro what happened to the dead bodies after she performed special treatments. Where did the bodies go? Curiosity mounted Ti Jocelyne and did not let go.

On her street neighbors were obsessed with the mirrored windows on a resplendent green SUV parked in the intersection. Ti Jocelyne rearranged the grocery bags on her shoulders and plunged into the depth of the crowd. One of the little boys shrieked:

"A white lady is here to see you!"

"A white lady?"

It was bizarre; she didn't know any white people. She sold handcrafted goods to white people in front of the hotels, but none of those people knew her name, let alone where she lived.

Ti Jocelyne abandoned the crowd for her corridor. Didoune stood above a pot of boiling green plantain halves. A pungent scent of French perfume merged with the smell of cooked food and made her nauseous. The source of her foregone nightmares was near. Ti Jocelyne found Madan Maurice seated on the white plastic chair next to Didoune's mattress. She froze and wasn't sure what to say. Didoune read Ti Jocelyne's face. Ti Jocelyne never discussed her childhood, but Didoune, like everyone else in Haiti, knew that *restavèk* children suffered immeasurable forms of degradation. Jessica's light complexion came from somewhere and the arrival of the green eyed woman revealed whence they came.

"*Madan*, can I serve you something? We have some chicken and onions in sauce and a bit of plantains and avocados, if you like." Didoune said.

Madan Maurice judged the meager accommodations and declined.

"I'm fine with the coffee you gave me."

Ti Jocelyne placed her mismatched assembly of plastic grocery bags in a corner and shot a glance meant to kill Madan Maurice.

"You really have no shame to come to a person's house without being invited. Who invited you to come here? I don't need any evil spirits here. I'll have to sweep and light candles when you leave so we're not invaded by your *lwa malfektè*."

Ti Jocelyne never thought about Madan Maurice since being kicked out of her house seven years ago. Her anger was calm and collected. Madan Maurice treated poor people like shit underneath her shoes and Ti Jocelyne was not about to debase herself.

"What did I do?" Madan Maurice asked with bewilderment "I took in a girl without a mother and gave her a place to live, taught her how to cook, how to clean, how to take care of a house, as if she were my own daughter. I taught you everything I know."

"I was your slave. At seven years old. I was your slave, nothing more. You never even paid me. Ten years, I worked in your house. You never gave me a *gourde*. You never sent me to school. Nothing."

Madan Maurice turned red as she wiped falling tears.

"How can you say that? You're the mother of my granddaughter. My only granddaughter, she's the child of my child."

"This is the first time I'm hearing my daughter has a grandmother. My mother died when I was seven years old. My child doesn't have a grandmother."

"When the child asks for her father, what do you tell her?"

"I tell her the truth. He's not here."

"No, you're right. He's not here. He's at the University of Florida working on his last diploma in engineering."

"You know what? We're not friends. Let's not pretend. Why are you here?" Ti Jocelyne snapped.

"You're a mother. So, when I tell you that my son is sick, you should understand. He has a type of cancer, where the treatment is found in the blood of the bones of his family." Madan Maurice explained, "I tried, his father, all of his cousins, aunts and uncles. None of us were a match." Madan Maurice said while tears flooded.

"What do you want from me?"

"I wanted to know if we could test your daughter to see if she is a possible match."

"Your shamelessness is stronger than you are. My daughter was born seven years ago. You put me out on the street after you caught your son forcing himself on me. Instead of correcting your son, you threw me out knowing I had nowhere else to go. The vendors, the street vendors, the coconut vendor, the fish woman, the mango merchant, they helped me. The same people you despised, do you remember how you used to send me to the market every day because you couldn't stand the scent of them? Well, it was those poor people who helped me-- not well-heeled people like you. They introduced me to someone who gave me a job. They introduced me to Didoune. Yes. This same Didoune you see right here, she didn't have more than two simple rooms and a back courtyard, but it was a royal palace because of how she treated me and my daughter."

Tears overwhelmed Madan Maurice and forced Didoune to shed empathetic tears.

"I ask you to pardon me. Pardon me. You don't need to hold whatever I did against you in your heart. What do you need? Anything you need, I will get it for you."

Ti Jocelyne had won. She needed nothing from Madan Maurice. Working for Gwo Pierro made her believe in her own power. Her responsibilities under Gwo Pierro had grown substantially over the last year. She hadn't had to ask anyone for charity in seven years. Her happiness in no longer needing Madan Maurice turned into distress. What would happen when Gwo Pierro died? He had no wife, no children. She didn't know anything about how the business worked. Ti Jocelyne was afraid. What would become of them when Gwo Pierro died? It would be difficult to get another job. Ti Jocelyne had never learned to read. Didoune didn't know how to read either. Ti Jocelyne could hear Gwo Pierro's faithful voice:

"Don't do zero. Don't do zero. Don't do zero."

She pushed these thoughts deep inside as Madan Maurice cried in the plastic chair. Don't do zero. Gwo Pierro introduced this idea when she was a scared pregnant teenager-- it had saved her life. Don't do zero. Life is a never ending series of negotiations. Even if you hate the person, or the person is evil, don't allow pride or scorn to prevent you from taking the food, clothing, shelter or help you need to survive. A blessing, even from an evil person, is still a blessing.

Madan Maurice was in Ti Jocelyne's home begging for a favor, the least Ti Jocelyne could do was get the highest asking price. Ti Jocelyne handed Madan Maurice a paper napkin from a plastic bag where she stashed reused Styrofoam plates and plastic utensils.

"You don't need to cry. I'm not God and I'm not here to judge you. As for money, we will talk about that later. What I want is an American passport for my daughter. Your son was born in Miami. All of you have American passports, I've seen them with my own two eyes. I want my daughter to have one too. So she can come and go as the ideas in her head tell her." Ti Jocelyne said plainly.

"But you need a birth certificate, and you need to file paperwork with the American government."

"*Eh bien.* You aren't as powerful as you pretend to be. The miserable and the poor are able to get forged birth certificates in every lost hole throughout the countryside, and you're telling me you can't get a birth certificate with her real father's name?"

"But it's not so easy. They may also want a blood test to prove that he is the father." Madan Maurice sighed.

"Well it falls perfectly. You need blood from Jessica and the Americans need blood from your son to prove that he is Jessica's father. Tap your behind twice to make it happen."

Jessica walked in with muddied feet. The neighborhood children were chasing a goat until she fell on a broken sidewalk chunk. Madan Maurice smiled through her puffy face and patted the stool next to her.

"Come and sit next to me. You can call me Mami Maurice."

Didoune stood with a concerned face.

"Do you smell burnt rubber?"

"I smell it too." Madan Maurice quipped.

The scent of burnt rubber meant one thing: political upheaval. Tak, tak, tak, tak, tak, tak, tak, tak, tak. A cascade of the gunshots brought additional fear.

Ti Jocelyne retrieved a ten thousand dollar bundle underneath the wooden latrine flap. Her hunch was correct; no one lingers by the latrine. She secured the cash to the small of her back with an old pair of pantyhose beneath her flowing cotton dress. The other half of her money was buried in a blue Danish cookie tin on a slanted ridge of witch's corner.

"We have to go. We don't need to be here for whatever is going to happen." Madan Maurice yelled.

Gunshots approached. Ti Jocelyne wasn't interested in what others were doing. She never followed politics and had no idea why the different political factions were constantly fighting. Jessica and Didoune were her concern. The increased gunshots got louder. Lost in mind and soul, fear surrounded her. She didn't know what to do and one person gave the most faithful counsel: Gwo Pierro.

Ti Jocelyne was certain that he could guide them through this. Her cell phone was hidden in a duct taped shoe box. It had one number saved. The phone's battery was dead. Neighbors connected an illegal extension cord into the EDH main power line across the hidden length of block. She would need to climb the back court wall to charge the phone. She didn't need much electricity. They cooked with charcoal and lit both small rooms with kerosene lamps. There were no televisions or refrigerators. Food was eaten before it considered spoiling. Siphoned electricity powered her cell phone and Didoune's radio.

Tak, tak, tak, tak, tak, tak, tak, tak, tak, tak. The sound of gunshots flew heavily outside. There was no time to charge her phone. It was time to go but she needed a *taptap* van. Shooting meant *taptap* vans would be packed or not running. Ti Jocelyne's head spun in several directions. What was going on at the church? How about the kids playing in the streets?

She was grateful Jessica had scraped her knees before the rioting.

Madan Maurice blocked the entranceway.

"You might as well come in my car. You won't be safe walking through this mess."

Ti Jocelyne hesitated. Madan Maurice was evil and prone to violent outbursts but today she wasn't the immediate threat-- random flying bullets were. Gwo Pierro's voice repeated in her head:

"Don't do zero. Don't do zero."

The devil she knew was better than the devil she didn't know. Ti Jocelyne, Didoune, Jessica and Madan Maurice passed through the wobbly corridor into the green SUV. Madan Maurice placed her key into the ignition.

"Where can we go if they are shooting like this? The road back to my house is blocked."

"I know where we can go, it is a guarded compound on the edge of town."

The SUV left the running crowd in its rearview mirror. Madan Maurice maintained her composure as Ti Jocelyne gave her directions.

Arriving at the compound gate, Madan Maurice assumed Ti Jocelyne worked as a maid for whoever lived inside. She honked the horn obnoxiously. Gwo Pierro stepped onto the balcony, saw Ti Jocelyne and instructed Sophie to open the door. Madan Maurice didn't hesitate to drive into the compound. Ti Jocelyne exited the car and opened the back door for Jessica. Gwo Pierro was waiting at the front door.

Holding back tears that were fighting to be unleashed, Ti Jocelyne quivered:

"They're burning and shooting in town. I don't know what's going on; we left as soon as we could and drove straight here."

"You don't have to be afraid. You're safe now." Gwo Pierro welcomed Ti Jocelyne and Jessica in an all-encompassing hug.

Ti Jocelyne had never felt this safe before. Gwo Pierro was her hope as the city turned towards disorder. Gwo Pierro recognized Madan Maurice as Jessica's grandmother.

"Sophie!" Gwo Pierro called out "Come and set up a space for you and the ladies in the shed. Take food, water, towels, pillows and anything else you'll need. It's made out of concrete. I'll leave you a couple of guns. Spirits are descending upon us. You don't have to worry, I will handle them. But, during times like these little vagabonds take advantage to ransack and rape. Don't come out until the noise stops. If any *ti vakabon* even looks at you the wrong way, you have my permission to throw two bullets his way."

"But how did you know?" Ti Jocelyne asked.

"My people have been calling me non-stop since this morning. They are here to get me. I'm ready and waiting for them."

Sophie, the ever hyper-organized housekeeper, had an encyclopedic knowledge of where everything was stored in Gwo Pierro's house. She quickly pulled together supplies. Ti Jocelyne, Madan Maurice and

Didoune carried large jugs of water, plastic bowls of food out of the refrigerator and a basket of ripe mangoes from the counter. Sophie reached into the laundry closet for freshly washed sheets and handed Jessica small pillows from the sofa.

The mosaic facade on the shed structure was covered with tiny white, beige, and grey pebbles.
The women carried as much as they could to huddle together into the shed. With the ladies safely inside, Gwo Pierro handed a gun to Sophie and closed the door.

"Lock the door and push the shelves against the door and window. Only come out when you hear no more noise." Gwo Pierro explained with a spirit of self-composure.

Sophie locked the door. Gwo Pierro banged on the door and yelled:

"Courage!"

Distinctions of class and color melted under the scorching prospect of mass shootings. The women pushed the sides of the heavy metal shelves towards the window. The shelving held tools, paint cans, antifreeze, cable wiring and household maintenance supplies. They pulled another shelf against the rear window. Jessica sat quietly in the corner biting her nails. It was a horrible habit but Ti Jocelyne wasn't about to interrupt her in the middle of this crisis. Her daughter was scared and if biting her nails calmed her down, so be it. Didoune was sweating excessively and Ti Jocelyne suggested opening the sheets on the shed floor so Didoune could stretch out. The commotion of the day was entirely too much for her older body to endure. Ti Jocelyne didn't care about making Madan Maurice comfortable in the least bit. Ti Jocelyne needed her alive to send in Jessica's American passport paperwork, nothing more, nothing less.

Each woman settled into a spot on the shed floor, Sophie took out a book and read silently. Ti Jocelyne admired Sophie's delightful state of peace and vowed that she would learn how to read when this upheaval was over. Sophie remained calm in the adversity at hand and Ti Jocelyne asked:

"What are you reading?"

"It's *Le Comte de Monte Cristo*. Gwo Pierro's favorite story of all time."

"Of course, it's a lovely story that everyone really should read." Madan Maurice blurted out.

Ti Jocelyne was astonished at how rich people always gave their opinion so freely, without being asked.

"Well, I worked as *restavèk* as a child and was never allowed to go to school, so I never learned to read." Ti Jocelyne responded.

Madan Maurice was silenced. Truth had a way of cutting through arrogance and pretension unlike no other weapon. Sophie sensed the tension in the shed and interjected:

"There's no problem. You can come here and I'll teach you how to read. Gwo Pierro is the best boss and he encourages me to read as many books as I can."

"You're right. Gwo Pierro is a great boss." Ti Jocelyne answered.

"You work for Gwo Pierro too?" Sophie seemed surprised. She thought she knew everyone who worked at Gwo Pierro's pharmacies and everyone who planned his events.

"I was asking myself, how do you know the man?" Madan Maurice chimed in.

"He sends me to run services for him on weekends." Ti Jocelyne responded.

Sophie didn't ask any additional questions because she figured it concerned Gwo Pierro disappearing during the weekends. Didoune could sense a change in the air and asked Sophie to read the *Count of Monte Cristo* aloud to help pass the time.

"No problem. I can read some pages if it helps keep everyone calm."

Sophie read the French text fluidly and without reservation. The words sounded different to Ti Jocelyne. The only place she ever heard French was at church. Sophie didn't read with the same sing-song tone that Pastor Jeremiah used during his sermons, nor did she quote from biblical passages that Ti Jocelyne had memorized years ago. She understood most of what Sophie read but couldn't pinpoint why or how the words were different. Ti Jocelyne lost herself in the images conjured by Sophie's voice until a barrage of bullets snapped them back into reality.

Sophie closed the book and instructed the women to huddle closer together as heavy gunshot rounds encircled the compound.

# 14 SAMANTHA SAVIN

*Miami Beach, Florida*

Samantha snapped pictures from inside of the car as they pulled into the Divitiae Pharma parking lot. Chris showed his badge and drove past the police barricade. Chris anchored his right arm behind Samantha's headrest to reverse into an empty spot before placing the shift stick into park.

Dead bodies were everywhere. Chris pulled a wrinkled nylon Miami Beach PD jacket out of the trunk. Samantha opened the passenger side door and slid her arm through the jacket sleeve. She nudged Chris and pointed her lips towards Rodriguez.

Samantha was overwhelmed by the blood soaked parking lot and couldn't catch her breath. Samantha and Chris tiptoed over dead bodies as Rodriguez guided them through the next set of police barriers. Several news helicopters circled above the scene to capture raw footage. The aerial noise on made it difficult to think. She needed quiet but there was none. One helicopter directed its glaring light into her face. Samantha exhaled her fear.

Ambulances lined the building entrances. One officer was charged with covering the bodies with black tarps. The sight of bile and human filth no longer made Samantha queasy; she had worked with cholera patients. But there was something about these dead powdered bodies in bloody puddles of filth that made her legs weak. Samantha snuck a deep breath when Chris became visibly unsettled at the sight of blood. It was the first time she had ever seen Chris nervous. Rodriguez caught Chris while he lost his nerve and the contents of his stomach. He snapped his fingers repeatedly to center Chris's attention.

"This is crazy." Samantha sympathized.

"How was I supposed to know?" Chris responded.

"Whatever" speaking softly to Samantha "Chris shouldn't have brought you here. You don't need to see this. It's too much."

"I work here. I've been trying to call my co-workers this morning and I haven't been able to reach anyone. I called the different company lines and nothing."

"Then you definitely shouldn't be here right now." Rodriguez countered.

"She can show us around the building and everything that's inside. OK?" Chris said curtly.

"I thought you said she was a doctor?"

"Doctorate in microbiology, research. I've been working here at Divitiae Pharma for the last few months."

"Oh, then help us wrap our heads around some of the bodies we found." Rodriguez gave in.

"Whatever you want to know."

From a distance, Samantha saw an older white cop on his phone frantically swatting away bugs while shouting into his phone.

Chris pinched her elbow and said:

"That's my boss I was telling you about."

"Oh, OK." Samantha scanned the dead bodies that were scattered over the asphalt and it was obvious that Chris's boss had no idea how to handle this catastrophe. Rodriguez tapped Sclafani on the shoulder.

"Boss, Chris brought an employee of the Divitiae Pharma Company to help us identify the bodies."

"Well done." Sclafani covered the end of the phone. "I have the Governor's office on the phone, I'll give them this update."

The three of them trod through the bloody site while Rodriguez lifted tarp covers one body at a time.

The first was excessively gored; she had been a middle aged Asian woman wearing a green dress but entire chunks of her face were missing and the rest was covered in congealed blood. They moved to the next body. Samantha let out an audible gasp and tears rolled.

"It's Janet, the receptionist. It's Janet." Samantha placed her face in Chris's chest.

"Maybe we should do this later?" Rodriguez suggested.

Samantha wiped away her tears.

"Their families deserve to know." Samantha insisted. "I have to call my mother and let them know I'm alright."

There were twenty seven missed calls on Samantha's phone. There was no time to answer everyone individually. She updated Facebook:

"Hey, Fam & Friends. I'm safe and will call everyone back as soon as I can. Love and light."

Chris hugged Samantha and wiped away her tears in front of his colleagues. Samantha was safe. He placed his arm around Samantha's shoulder and led her through the next set of corpses. Some were familiar and others were strangers. Rodriguez pulled back another tarp and Samantha saw her boss, Drew Michaels. His dead body was drenched in blood and shit. Police bullets ravaged his chest with broken rib bones and intestines exposed.

Samantha was with him on Thursday afternoon. She wasn't in the office on Friday, he sent her to represent the department at the University of Miami Special Seminar Series. He wanted everyone to shine and encouraged his junior staff to build their professional reputations. Samantha was scheduled to debrief him on Monday. It was Sunday morning and it was too late.

Samantha's heart dropped. Did she still have a job? Her department head was dead, this was his research. What would his death mean for her? Samantha felt selfish and heartless as she stood over her colleagues' dead bodies.

She forced another deep breath and hummed her mantra:

"Beauty and terror happen. Keep going. Beauty and terror happen. Keep going. Beauty and terror happen. Keep going."

Samantha got this job without any special hook-ups or favors; if she had too, she would find another job. Ideas sputtered inside her head. Before Samantha could get completely lost in her thoughts, Rodriguez unveiled more dead bodies until she had seen every dead face. She stood in a trance when Captain Sclafani approached her.

"Would you be able to draw an outline of the facility? We haven't been able to get through to anyone. Divitiae Pharma's lawyers told us intellectual property issues were at stake and that a statement is coming. What the fuck am I supposed to do with a statement when I've got all these dead bodies?"

Samantha hated bullshit. Cops were not a rival pharmaceutical company, even if they showed them every single book or formula on file-- the cops wouldn't understand anything. It's like hiding porn magazines from the blind. It made no sense. Samantha hated needless red-tape. Mourning families shouldn't be forced to suffer when TV cameras made the bloody truth plain.

Samantha entered Divitiae Pharma and all of her projects, tests, forms, meetings and conversations over the last four months bombarded her. She scoured her mind as to what could have caused any of this because none of it made sense.

Sclafani joined the three of them in the building.

"And here I thought, oh, I'm just going to take it easy for the next fourteen months until retirement. No fuckin way that's gonna happen now. Why can't the world come to a goddamn end on someone else's watch?" Sclafani lowered his voice as the blood rushed to his head. "OK. Young lady tell me what the hell this company does every day apart from making aspirin. Cuz, I may not be the sharpest knife in the drawer but I know aspirin can't cause shit like this."

"I can't speak for every other department. It's a large company."

"Then give me the Wikipedia version. Who is in charge, what does he do?" Sclafani responded.

"Divitiae Pharma is the third most profitable pharmaceutical company in the world. It was founded by John van Holst over fifty years ago when he was a broke young chemical engineering graduate coming out of Florida State. He started his company with effective medicinal patents, basic vaccines and then made a fortune on chemotherapy and other cancer treatments, he was one of the first to delve into stem cell research, and right now, Divitae Pharma is the foremost leader in gene drive technology. He's been on Forbes's top ten rich list for the last twenty years."

"Now, tell me, what you do every day?"

"My department is responsible for gene drive technology experiments."

"What for?" Rodriguez interrupted.

"Applications of gene drive include preventing the spread of diseases carried by mosquitoes or ticks that transmit malaria, dengue, and zika pathogens or to control invasive species, or to eliminate resistance. The technique can be used to change genes to cause a crash in certain insect populations by reducing their reproductive capacity."

"You're trying to reprogram bugs?" Sclafani asked.

"Essentially, yes, with the understanding that there could be an incredible upside for human beings if we succeed in changing the genetic structures of certain insects."

"I don't know what any of this means and it's way too complicated for me. All I know is I've got six cops who were forced to leave over two dozen dead bodies in your company parking lot. It's not even noon and I need some whiskey."

Rodriguez cleared his throat.

"Captain, we are in the building now. The other officers have secured the entire location. Let our guys review the security tapes, Chris can go with Samantha to inspect her office for anything out of the ordinary. Go ahead and call the higher ups. Tell the staffers from the Mayor and Governor's offices that we'll share security tapes footage with them in a couple of hours."

Sclafani answered his phone and walked away.

"I love the old guy, but this is gonna kill him. It's too much stress for him. Tell me exactly what they are doing in here again." Chris said.

In Samantha's lab, Chris and Rodriguez photographed files, petri dishes, cages, flasks and the general workspace.

"What were you guys working on specifically? Every day, you would come in, get a cup of coffee, check your email, check Instagram, then what?" Rodriguez asked as Samantha searched through a stack of papers.

"The research concerned our ability to change the order in certain genes. Most recently, the team was working on curbing the ability of mosquitoes to spread diseases like Zika, malaria or Lone Star Tick meat allergy.

"Are you serious? People are getting tick bites and can't eat chicken wings after that?"

"Well, not exactly. In this example, people developed allergies to beef, lamb, pork, and goat." Samantha answered.

"Goat? Who's eating goat in Texas?"

"Well, there are plenty of Nigerian and Caribbean immigrants in Texas and throughout the south. It seems that the allergy affects the consumption of mammals. People who displayed characteristics of the allergy were still able to eat fish and chicken without suffering the adverse physical triggers."

"What was the end game? What would have gotten you the bonus come December?" Rodriguez asked.

"Finding a way to change the genetic sequence so people who are bitten by the tick no longer develop allergies to red meat."

Chris reentered the lab upset.

"I had the forensic team play some of the footage from Friday and it's crazy. Was there a party here on Friday?"

"I mean, not a party, but yes, a barbecue. They always grill hamburgers and hot dogs in the company backyard, that's what they do every time they celebrate something. At least once a month, wine and beer, burgers and franks and then a Costco cake."

As the newest staffer, Samantha was assigned the exposed desk next to the door. No matter how she rearranged the seat or computer, her screen remained visible to anyone who came into the lab. Samantha searched through shelves, random boxes and bins around her desk unsure of what she was looking for. At first, she wasn't able to find the last group of sequences from the departmental report. Samantha scattered papers and dug through the color coded files until she found two identical flash drives. She put them in her pocket to sort through at home and sat on the edge of the rolling chair to search through her bottom desk drawer. Her left hand leaned on the armrest and a cool chalk powder remained on her palm.

Samantha rolled her chair closer to the desk. A faint coat of white powder covered the entire end of the laboratory. The light dusting of powder had missed the front end of the workspace, but it was visible on the other upholstered mint green chairs. Samantha counted four air vents in the ceiling. She led Chris and Rodriguez to the heaviest concentration of white powder.

"The powder, it gets denser the further you walk into the lab."

The powder was everywhere and a light dusting covered the computer screens and the glass sterilization enclosures. On the counter, half eaten burgers were left on small plates at different workstations. Samantha shielded her nose with her arm.

"Don't touch anything. Let's get out of here. We need to identify the contents of the powder."

Rodriguez covered his mouth with the top of his shirt before exiting on his right heel:

"You don't have to tell me twice.

Chris pushed Samantha by the small of her back out of the laboratory.

"Don't you want to grab any files?"

"No, I don't know what any of this powder is and I'm not bringing it back home with me. I have remote access to my work hardrive and I can access everything that I was working on from home. I have no idea what this powder is."

"What, you think it's like anthrax?" Chris asked.

"I have no idea what it is. We'll need to change our clothes and wash our hands before we get into the car." Samantha insisted.

"I have workout clothes in my gym bag in the car. You can wear those. I'll ask one of the other cops for another jacket and a uniform from the back of one of the station cars." Chris replied.

On their way out of the Divitiae Pharma, Chris introduced Samantha to Habib, one of the forensic IT guys Chris played video games with during work hours. Habib gave Chris a handshake that concealed his transfer of an external hard drive.

Samantha saw Chris discreetly placed something the size of a deck of cards in his pocket without asking any questions. High profile cases attracted politicians while state and federal investigators sought opportunities to override local police departments. Chris and Habib had an established system of making copies of evidence footage in the event shit ever hit the fan. Samantha, wary of police, figured that if Habib gave Chris the video footage, it meant that the cops were telling the truth. It was a form of insurance if anyone ever came for them. If some attorney or politician made damning speeches or tried to sell the police department out, they could unearth previously unreleased video footage to embarrass camera hungry elected officials.

A million thoughts ran through Samantha's head. What was the powder? What happened to the people? Why so much blood? She didn't have the necessary equipment to run tests on the powder at home but she needed to find the answers.

Samantha and Chris moved into the crowded main entrance where dead bodies remained flat on the asphalt. She fixated on the powder. It was spread throughout the blood drenched dead bodies. Chris tapped the small of her back before leaving her to speak to Captain Sclafani, already in a conversation with a man Samantha recognized as Spencer Warren, chief of staff to Divitiae Pharma's Chairman: John van Holst.

Spencer Warren served as the host of the internal company quarterly meeting a couple of months ago where the Chairman encouraged staffers to give their all to the company. They were partners in the creation of a new world. Samantha remembered how enamored her co-workers were while watching the chairman deliver his remarks; he had created the company out of nothing and was still as sharp as a tack, even though his body grew increasingly frail with each passing year. Most impressive was the Chairman's ability to embrace technology and innovation in his nineties. He was seated on a hovering chair without wheels. He belonged to this new millennium even though his wrinkles and shaky voice testified to being born in the last one. The Chairman maintained high spirits and had an effortless manner of motivating his staff to prioritize company goals ahead of their individual petty pursuits.

His chief of staff, Spencer Warren, wore a light blue oxford shirt, crisp khakis and projected calm as he spoke with Captain Sclafani. Samantha watched from a distance as Chris joined their conversation. Investigators were managing the scene and had mounted temporary green and blue canopy structures to keep the sun and helicopter cameras off of the crime scene. Samantha recognized him, but he had no idea she existed. Spencer Warren had never spoken to Samantha and the probability of him knowing an entry-level researcher was nil.

# 15 GWO PIERRO

*Okap, Haiti*

Gunshots raced up the road. Alex Duperville wanted control of the North of Haiti and Gwo Pierro was the last obstacle. Northern decision makers, press contacts, business leaders, supporters and friends would be impossible for Alex to control with Gwo Pierro alive.

Gwo Pierro was astonished by Alex's stupidity. Telephones have been tapped in Haiti since the 1960's. Alex Duperville's cell phone conversations were monitored. Power or not, spells or not, Alex had failed to take the simple precautions of any self-respecting leader. It was easy for Gwo Pierro to pay someone at the cell company to transcribe Alex's calls. The source of Gwo Pierro's influence was that he invested in people years before he needed a favor. When a street kid built a walkie-talkie out of batteries, busted headphones and old telephone parts, he paid that kid's registration fees from junior high school through to university. Gwo Pierro handed him a way forward. Working in the telephone company's engineering department, he was ecstatic to do anything for Gwo Pierro.

Gwo Pierro prospered year after year because he avoided politics. He saw countless men fall on their faces trying to become president. It never interested him. Neither did having power for power's sake. Gwo Pierro gave politicians bribes and was happy to be rid of them. Alex Duperville wanted power. His family's connections and vetiver processing fortune were no longer enough. Alex wanted to achieve power on a global scale. But first Alex needed two things: increased access to capital and a consolidation of vital stakeholders in Okap.

Informants revealed that Alex intended to exploit the gold mines at Morne Bossa. The mines were barely six miles outside Okap. To control the mines, Alex would need unmitigated control of the power brokers in Okap to coordinate trucks, water access, digging supplies, security and ancillary trade considerations within the region. Lingering property claims by small tenant farmers and bourgeois families would need to be squashed. Alex intended to strong arm the region into submission while giving required crumbs to government officials.

Mining experts had estimated that as much as twenty billion dollars' worth of gold in Morne Bossa was waiting to be exploited. Hillary Clinton's brother Tony joined the board of directors of Delaware based VCS Mining which was granted one of two licenses to exploit and export the gold outside of Haiti in 2012. Alex was preparing his zombies to work the mines. It would mean free labor and increased security. Zombies can't tell family and friends about the wealth hidden in Haiti, nor would they try to steal the gold for themselves. It was a win-win solution for Alex, an army of zombies to make his dream of absurd wealth and power a reality. Alex was no longer content to be rich by Haitian standards; he aspired to join the billionaires of the global elite.

A government permit in Haiti meant absolutely nothing if the people on the ground weren't getting a couple of dollars to line their pockets. Gwo Pierro saw Hillary Clinton's brother at an event in Haiti back in 2012 and understood that no good could come from having the Clintons involved with gold exploitation in Haiti. The collateral damage would cost too much. It would take thirty years to exploit twenty billion in gold with the government getting eight hundred million. Every year the Haitian diaspora sends two billions dollars home. There was no way VCS Mining, Tony Rodham or even Alex Duperville would be able to get the gold out of Haiti without killing entire towns. Alex's army of zombies represented the first round of bloodshed.

Alex Duperville belonged to the most influential *bòkò* secret society in Haiti: Galère. Composed of ten members, one *bòkò* was responsible for issues affecting a different region in Haiti. Hillary Clinton was due to receive her own recompense. In the aftermath of the devastating 2010 earthquake, the Clinton Foundation received almost a billion dollars in donations to help Haiti rebuild. The Clintons were never able to account for hundreds of millions of dollars donated by people across the world.

The Galère called a plenary session to resolve the Clinton matter. The Clintons had honeymooned in Haiti in the seventies but Haitians believed that the young couple went to Haiti seeking power spells to secure the American presidency. Locals throughout Haiti, from mountainside to hillside, peasants and pastors alike, were convinced that the Clintons had long ago signed over their souls in Vodou ceremonies. How else could they account for the Clintons' constant visits to Haiti throughout the years? Bill and Hillary, like others before them, forgot that they had signed away their souls to a Galère *bòkò* in exchange for political power.

The last time they called such a meeting it was to have Aristide removed from power in 2004, they had remained neutral in his previous removal by coup d'etat in 1991. This time, the Galère met to ensure that Hillary Clinton would never become president of the United States.

They held their meeting on October 17, 2016, on Dessalines Day in Gonaïves. They collectively conjured the spirit of Dessalines to, *pour le pays, pour les ancêtres*, castigate and rid Haiti of the spirit of the Clintons forever. They had done too much, failing to account for money that was meant for poverty stricken Haitians was horrible enough, but having a useless brother associated with the potential exploitation of twenty billion dollars' worth of gold out of Haiti was not to be borne. If anyone was going to exploit twenty billion dollars' worth of gold out of Haiti, it was going to be them.

On the evening of November 8, 2016, Hillary watched the presidency slip between her fingers. With Hillary out of power, her brother's company exploit permit was worthless -- leaving a perfect opening for Alex Duperville to gain access over the gold mines in Morne Bossa.

Members of the Galère were the few on the island who understood the depth of Gwo Pierro's strength as a *houngan*. None of the spells that the Galère cast on Gwo Pierro ever worked. Enough was enough. It was time to get rid of Gwo Pierro so that Alex and the Galère could gain unfettered control of the north, its gold mines and place one of their own at the helm of the Haitian presidency.

Gwo Pierro sensed Alex Duperville and released one powerful suck of his teeth:

"Tschrrrrrrp."

Rage rose in Gwo Pierro. Alex awakened the spirits that lived within him. Gwo Pierro hated fighting; it left him depleted; the internal warning of an oncoming fight stirred the spirit in his limbs and head. There was no avoiding it. If he wanted to protect the lives of everyone under his care, he would have to fight Alex Duperville from the core.

Gwo Pierro prepared to fight Alex by invoking his own council members. Alex Duperville inherited his seat on the Galère council from his father. Unlike anything inherited, Gwo Pierro cultivated his own council of *mambos* across Haiti. Whereas the Galère were all men, and their seats were passed down from father to son over the last two hundred years, Gwo Pierro selected each *mambo* based on their raw spiritual energy and geographical location. True power in Haiti existed in the wombs of nameless women in distant towns and hillsides--- not in security barricaded villas. Gwo Pierro had 417 *mambos* positioned strategically around Haiti, women he nurtured over the last thirty years, as he had nurtured Ti Jocelyne and Sophie. His council members lived in towns along the periphery of Haiti and generated a spiritual force field around the entirety of their territory.

The 417 women who transferred their power to Gwo Pierro, lived in forgotten towns, some in huts, and others in houses. Gwo Pierro had drawn a powerful redline around the circumference of Haiti years ago, he had a *mambo* in Savane Zombie, Foret des Pins, Fonds-Verrettes, Mallepasse, Ganthier, Cottin, Decayette, Cornillon, Rato, St. Pierre, Gros Figure, Bois Marin, Bois Cochon, Belladere, El Bay, Metalac, Thomassique, Nan Pomme, Cerca La Source, Bois de Laurence, Liane Panier, Mont-Organise, Capotille, Acul de Pins, Perrier, Gillote, Derac, Fort Liberte-, Phaeton, Caracol, Samson, Quartier-Morin, Nan Blanque, Bas Limbe, St. Michel, Anse a Foleur, Deboucher, Port-de-Paix, Gros-Bassin, Callbassier, Nan Digo, Mole St. Nicolas, Faligon, Chillote, La Plateforme, Baie-de-Henne, Anse-Rouge, Corridor, Ti Saline, Lataniere, Gonaive, Nan Piguel, Grande-Saline, Dugazon, Saint Marc, Anse a Pirogue, Pierre Payen, Deloge, Augier, Montrouis, Kat-Kalen, Marotte, Dasse, Mitan, Merotte, Archahaie, Garache, Ballelle, Lafiteau, Basat, Minelas, Cite- Soleil, Fort Dimanche, Carrefour, Gressier, Lafferonay, La Salle, Pandou, Cheridan, Pitan, Brossier, Cassagne, Buteau, La Coudre, Grand Trout, Mayombe, Grand Goave, Petit-Goave, Port Royal, Miragoane,… and hundreds of other bends marking the geographical and spiritual outline of Haiti.

After defeating Alex Duperville at Lababee Beach, Gwo Pierro called his ultimate line of defense: his council *mambos*. They cast protection spells and summoned spirits to safeguard Gwo Pierro from Alex Duperville.

The women Gwo Pierro cultivated over the last decades were washerwomen, street vendors, household maids, prostitutes, lesbians, and other women rejected by those around them. Gwo Pierro redeemed them one-by-one and enlisted them into his service. They were loyal to Gwo Pierro. He sent them money every month and clothes and perfume on their birthdays. Where lovers and husbands had failed, and parents had disappeared or died, Gwo Pierro was the positive presence in their lives.

There was no doubt that they would follow his instructions when they received the chain calls telling them to light their candles. Each woman had a cell phone and the number of three other women. All Gwo Pierro had to do was call one woman and tell her to light the candles for him at sunrise and she immediately called the next three women instructing them to do the same. Call after call, the women didn't stop calling until they had received at least three separate calls with the same message to protect Gwo Pierro. The protection spells poured forth until the burned candle wicks transported their prayers to the realm of the invisibles.

Gwo Pierro was prepared. Ti Jocelyne, Sophie, Didoune, Madan Maurice and little Jessica were protected in his shed. He stood patiently on his forged iron balcony and waited for Alex Duperville. Whooshing bullets grew closer. Gwo Pierro remained unmoved as a faint scent of talcum powder revealed itself. Large truck engines revved. Black canvas covered army trucks claimed the private road leading to the front gate of the compound. Thick clouds of dust ascended as the trucks gathered speed. Gwo Pierro was centered in peace.

The brown dust was replaced by a cloud of talcum powder which suffocated the street. When the cloud grew closer, Gwo Pierro saw Alex Duperville and an army of zombies behind him. There were at least two thousand of them girded in white loincloths and covered with talcum powder from head to toe. Marching an army of zombies through Okap was Alex Duperville's self-coronation as the supreme *bòkò* in Haiti. No one dared threaten an infantry of zombies, not governmental officials, not elite business owners, not superstitious peasants and certainly not shoeless laborers. Mouths were agape as a blatant regime change occurred before their eyes. Those who came out in the street to pray or lament the zombies were shot on sight. Even those who failed to find shelter quick enough were shot down by Alex Duperville's gunmen.

Alex Duperville corralled the zombies to fabricate his legend; a preemptive display of violence would solidify Alex's exploitation of the gold mines without political protests or community complaints. It was time to claim his rightful dominion over the seen and unseen in Haiti--- Gwo Pierro was the last obstacle in his way.

The trucks honked to a grinding halt at Gwo Pierro's gate. Alex Duperville came out of the black Suburban truck and mounted the hood of the vehicle. He pointed a machete at Gwo Pierro who was still waiting on the balcony.

"Come down now and I won't let the zombies devour you."

"Today is the last day you will breathe air on this earth." Gwo Pierro responded.

Gwo Pierro invoked the collective strength of the 417 women; he reclaimed the lost souls that Alex Duperville had stolen from the thousands of zombies that filled the streets of Okap. Gwo Pierro and the 417 women summoned the power of the invisibles:

*"Adjae, adjae, adjae, adjae, adjae, adjae, adjae, adjae, adjae, adjae…"*

Alex Duperville ordered the drivers to clear a path for the zombies. Some had eaten the flesh of stragglers as they passed through the local streets. Blood stained mouths drew a stark contrast on their talc covered black skin. The mass of zombies funneled through the trucks and landed on Gwo Pierro's front gate. Some clawed at the fence while others were trampled under the fervent mindlessness of soulless men marching into the barricade. The gate nearly collapsed under the weight of zombies. Alex shot a round into the sky to agitate the zombies. Gwo Pierro stood erect in his white linen and chanted:

*Yo dit bawon pa lwa l ye*
*Gade m konne c'est lwa l ye*
*Yo dit bawon pa lwa l ye*
*Gade m konne c'est lwa l ye*

Gwo Pierro shouted from the bottom of his soul and was lifted in a hypnotic trance. The chant had taken over. A centrifugal force spread his arms above the rest of his body and rotated him. From below, Alex Duperville and his men recognized that Gwo Pierro was not spinning on his own strength. Some scattered. Others fired useless shots.

The chant was in control. The spirit of Baron Samedi entered Gwo Pierro with each rotation. As each word left his lips, Gwo Pierro's sizeable plump flesh spun faster until he levitated off the balcony. The lightning fast spin propelled Gwo Pierro into the air. He floated above the mass of zombies with both hands facing the North Star which was temporarily hidden by the sun. Gwo Pierro pointed his arm north, then south, then west, then east and the dizzying circle carried him further into the sky.

*"Sa m pa wè yo, nò*
*Sa m pa wè yo, sid*
*Sa m pa wè yo, lwès*
*Sa'm pa wè yo, lès"*

*Those I cannot see, north*
*Those I cannot see, south*
*Those, I cannot see, west*

*Those, I cannot see, east*

Gwo Pierro galvanized so much electricity through his body that his curly hair stood straight. When Gwo Pierro stopped spinning, a blinding light emanated from Gwo Pierro. When he opened his eyes, additional light broke through. A raw power mounted his vessel and radiated through his fingertips and bare toes. The spirit of Baron Samedi had overtaken Gwo Pierro's body as he defied the laws of gravity. Alex Duperville's power was no match for Baron Samedi.

An uncontrollable current of fear hit Alex Duperville and he fell off the hood of his SUV as he shot aimlessly at Gwo Pierro hovering above. His men shot their guns with furor; their bullets seemed incapable of reaching Gwo Pierro. His body was suspended between their physical world and that of the spirits.

His Baron Samedi possessed body lowered his head and with one swift movement of his hands, confiscated the souls of the zombies from Alex Duperville's control. The thousands of zombies obeyed Gwo Pierro and with a flick of his wrist, the zombies turned to attack Alex Duperville and his hired gunmen.

The sheer weight of the mass of zombies broke the truck windows, leaving the gunmen vulnerable. One-by-one, the soulless men ate flesh to satisfy the insatiable hunger created by the theft of their souls.

The soulless zombies surpassed their natural understanding. As the zombies devoured everyone who had come to destroy Gwo Pierro, his body floated undisturbed. Alex hid underneath a SUV kicking away the zombies as he could. Gwo Pierro raised his left hand and a dozen of the zombies pushed the truck onto its side.

Exposed, Alex cried:

"*Mamman mwen, mamman mwen*"

"*My mother, my mother*"

It was too late; one zombie bit the side of his rib while another tore his neck with his talc covered mouth. Blood squirted everywhere until he was too weak to move. Alex was no more.

The barrier between the dead and the living was open. The spirits were separated from their bodies and the ethereal dimensions that made them invisible were gone. The zombies and the newly arrived spirits were equally visible to the plain eye. When the last living gunman's soul abdicated his body, Gwo Pierro faced north and raised his hands.

The mass of zombies pivoted on their heels towards the long winding private road. More steps moved them further north until they reached the main road. Gwo Pierro floated above them and ordered them onto Rue A. The zombies marched solemnly past the brightly painted houses and businesses of Okap. Townsfolk who respected Gwo Pierro as a gregarious businessman could no longer pretend. Gwo Pierro had hidden his position as the most powerful man in town. From inside their homes, through the glass window panes, it was impossible to hide the truth. The *lwa* of Baron Samedi was upon Gwo Pierro and wielded the key to the door between the living and the dead. With another hand motion, the lifeless partially eaten bodies of Alex Duperville and his hired gunmen rose from the depths of death to follow the zombies down Rue A.

People were petrified and hid in their homes and inhabited crevices. Their curiosity outweighed their fears; they peeked through cracks in doors, shutters and perforated concrete blocks. No one believed their eyes: Gwo Pierro levitated high above the ground while commanding a mass of zombies through town. There was a deafening sound of silence in Okap. Babies knew not to cry and dogs did not dare bark. Thousands of barefoot zombies marched and none made a sound. Gwo Pierro floated over them as they passed the radio station, an abandoned bakery, the Seventh- Day Adventist Church, Capital Bank, the gas stations, Unibank, Sogexpress, the Banque National de Credit, Bureau de la covention Baptiste d'Haiti, the Banque de la République d'Haiti, Banana Food Drink N More, All Systems Barbecue and more on Rue A until they reached Hotel Mont Joli. The mass of zombies glided by the remaining seafront restaurants and bars that converged Rue A into Boulevard du Cap-Haitien.

Gwo Pierro faced the sea. He levitated above as the mass of zombies met mounds of sand which invited them into the transparent sea. The horde of zombies entered the sea, each one taking his turn into the wet abyss until their heads were no longer seen. The thousands of soulless bodies disappeared into water at a steady pace until the only zombie left before Gwo Pierro was a flesh devoured frame that had once belonged to Alex Duperville. Gwo Pierro lowered himself from the sky, raised his hand and commanded Alex Duperville into the sea.

Baron Samedi fully dismounted Gwo Pierro when his bare feet touched the sand because it belonged to another spirit. Gwo Pierro raised his hand to salute the spirit of the sea--- Agwe.

"All go unto one place; all are of the sea and to the sea we all return

*M'ap rele Agwe oh*
*Grace oh*
*Oh Agwe, Oh Agwe*
*se mwen ki la oh!*
*M'ap rele Agwe oh"*

*I'm calling on Agwe oh*
*Grace oh*
*Oh Agwe Oh Agwe*
*I'm calling on Agwe oh*

*Ayibobo"*

# 16 CHRIS

*Miami Beach, Florida*

The police precinct was tense. There was no time to play video games. Sclafani, Chris's commanding officer, was short-tempered. Meetings with health department officials, federal and state oversight committees, and mandatory retraining sessions eviscerated morale. Sclafani was avoiding the press and ordered his cops to do the same. Six days after the killings, forms came from every direction. Chris feared Sclafani was about to crack.

He hated media attention and could barely handle Black Lives Matter activists in front of the station. They paled in comparison to the national spotlight on the department; twenty white pharmaceutical employees were shot dead by his cops. Security video footage was released within forty-eight hours and did nothing to quell the public outrage. Freeze frame images of one cop's face being chomped was already a meme. Television segments deconstructing the videos introduced a chorus of talking heads, law enforcement experts, academics and politicians eager to play armchair officer in exchange for free publicity. They should have used tasers? Couldn't they have shot bean bags instead of bullets? Why didn't they release tear gas?

Chris did his best to concentrate on the medical professionals and the physiological causes of such gruesome reactions. Were the people suffering from a psychosis? Did they have a disastrous reaction to a chemical within the lab? What were they processing in that lab? Different media outlets interviewed pathologists, psychologists, neurologists, drug experts and anyone else they could find to explain the cannibalistic carnage witnessed in the videos.

The Internet, never to be left out of the conversation, used a word that none of the journalists, political pundits or medical professionals dared utter in public: zombie. The memes and gifs warning of an oncoming zombie apocalypse were quickly discounted as preposterous. But in private, and when he was alone, Chris wondered if the bloody bodies investigated over the last few months could actually be zombies. He was attacked by a stripper that was strong beyond comprehension. Chris rewatched the video of the pharma workers attacking the police; their lack of consciousness was also framed by excessive strength.

Sclafani ordered Chris to review all of his case files from the past twelve months. Chris analyzed every witness list; he scoured phone records and double-checked any bit of information that he may have overlooked. Rodriguez, who had long ago delegated paperwork responsibilities to Chris, was elbow deep in files and forms. The pharmaceutical company was stonewalling behind a gang of the best attorneys in Florida. They refused to release an iota of information unless compelled by a judge. The more they resisted, the more Chris's suspicion grew.

Despite its international glamour, Miami Beach operated like a small town. The overlap between politicians, business owners, teachers, mechanics, waiters and beach bums meant there were two degrees of separation between locals. Whenever Chris met another local, the first order of business was to determine who they knew in common. Divitiae Pharma was less than three miles from the strip clubs where the first mutilated dead bodies were found. There had to be a connection. The pharma company continued to decline requests for information.

Arrogance blinded them. They forgot police can gain access to telephone records without their consent.

With Sclafani's approval, Chris obtained a court order to access Divitiae Pharma telephone records. He cross-referenced every telephone number coming in and out of the company against numbers linked to the mutilated death cases. There was a match: Nissar, the strip club manager.

Chris reread the files and fixated on Nissar's stripper Butta, who attacked him at Matt's bachelor party. His doubt disappeared. Nissar was connected to these killings. But he wasn't able to prove anything illegal occurred; the girls were over eighteen years old and he wasn't selling drugs. At most, he gifted drugs in exchange for sexual favors. He rang a number called several times over the last nine months.

"Hello, Mr. Warren's office." An older lady replied.

"Oh, good morning, I'm calling to speak with Paul Warren, please."

"Oh, I'm sorry this is Spencer Warren's office. I don't have a directory to transfer you to other company employees."

"Thank you, I'll send an email instead." Chris replied.

"Have a nice day."

Chris googled Spencer Warren and Divitiae Pharma. Countless hits appeared, including a Linkedin profile. He was in his mid-forties, preppy with parted hair, tie, and blazer. His profile listed him at Divitiae Pharma for the past thirteen years, and as chief-of-staff to the chairman for the last six years. He held an MBA from Harvard and a bachelor's degree in chemical engineering from MIT. Additional search results revealed he was a triathloner and traveled to Davos, Shanghai, São Paulo and Cape Town, all within the last six months.

What does a chief-of-staff do anyway? Which staff was he managing? Large corporations had chief executive officers, chief operating officers, chief finance officers, chief information officers and other c-level executives to run extensive ends of the business. Does a chief-of-staff manage c-level executives? The company's president? Corporate titles were confusing. He studied the Linkedin profile more carefully; it read 'Chief-of-Staff, Office of the Chairman'. Why would he call Nissar? Chris found a picture of the chairman online. The old man appeared younger than the ninety-six years listed on his Wikipedia page. Signs of the chairman's natural age were replaced by a taut lizard face shared by plastic surgery enthusiasts.

Nissar managed a strip club, maybe Spencer Warren liked to watch tits and ass. But the calls to the club from the office occurred between 10 a.m. and 3:00 p.m. Perhaps Nissar furnished a steady supply of young women to the old man. Women scheme to meet rich men, but even heartless gold diggers needed help to overcome the impossibilities of a ninety-six year old man. Dead gory bodies at Nissar's strip club and mutilated zombies at Divitiae Pharma were not a coincidence. Chris asked Rodriguez to join him in Sclafani's office.

"I'll tell you what. Those pharma bastards have billions and a troop of lawyers to hide behind, this Nissar guy doesn't have any of that. Bring him in." Sclafani said.

Chris and Rodriguez grabbed their belongings before tapping on the employee lounge glass door. Rodriguez poked in:

"We're going to the strip club to bring in a suspect for the shredded bodies. We need back-up."

Nine cops followed in separate vehicles; sirens blazed to the strip club to bring in Nissar. The cop cars attracted bystanders on the sidewalk who blocked the club entrance to get a glimpse of some action..

"Where is Nissar?" Chris asked.

"I don't know where anybody is. I'mma stand here, tryna to keep these crazy sickos in their seats. That's all I do. That's all I know. I got absolutely no idea what's going on in these other rooms. But you can go ahead and look for whoever inside." The tall Dominican bouncer said.

Two of the cops remained outside while the others went in. Male patrons were eating their lunch and watching asses shake. Another pair of cops secured the circular stage and locked eyes on strippers gyrating around the pole. Chris, Rodriguez and the other cops meandered into the hidden realm of the club that was painted shades of purple with touches of red with black and white leather lounge sofas and barstools. Black lights elicited uncontrollable reactions to the naked bodies, music, alcohol and drugs. Natural light encourages people to make good decisions. There was no source of natural light in the strip club. The hallway was also painted shades of purple and red, low lounge chairs hugged the walls, and invited quick stripper blow jobs.

Chris asked a random woman:

"Where is Nissar?"

"He should be in his office, last door in the back." The waitress answered.

They opened the door without knocking:

"Police! Police! Police! Police!"

The white walls enclosed natural wooden furniture and floors; the white sofa was soft to the touch. A window facing the alleyway welcomed the warm Miami sun. The room belonged in a magazine. Potted plants nestled the window pane and taller plants graced large pots in the corner. Chris and Rodriguez burst into the peaceful office. Nissar was seated at his desk with his shoulder length hair combed away from his face.

"How may I help you gentlemen?" Nissar asked.

"Stand slowly and place your hands above your head." Rodriguez screamed.

Nissar followed the instructions.

"Come from around the desk." Chris said.

As he was lowering his arms behind his back, Rodriguez placed handcuffs on Nissar's wrists while one of the other cops read his rights.

Chris sat at Nissar's desk. The computer was on a discount travel website. Chris searched through previous browser pages before opening his email. Nothing was out of the ordinary. It was full of store sales, reminders to pay his car insurance, and newspaper briefs. Chris concentrated on his erased emails. People forget to clear deleted emails. It was a ready-made package. There were dozens of emails, half of which were from the same person: Amina Duperville.

Email after email was in French. Chris struggled through Spanish in high school and was ill-equipped to decipher them. He forwarded himself Nissar's deleted emails. No one would listen to Nissar rant about first amendment rights with these bloody deaths. A judge's signature would be on the court order before they returned to the police precinct. Chris needed Samantha to translate them. The precinct translator, Officer Baptiste, liked to proselytize colleagues to death. There was no time for Baptiste today, nor did he have the mental energy to find a polite excuse. He had to find Samantha.

Nissar was driven to the precinct in the other police car. His colleagues would make him sweat in the cell for hours before interrogation. Everyone is a tough guy until those iron bars close. Sitting behind bars for a few hours would change his tone.

Chris texted Samantha:

"Where r u?"

"I'm at the temp lab preparing reports."

"Did u eat yet?"

"Nope."

"Ok. I'll get some sandwiches."

"🌶🌶🌶🌶🌶🌶"

He bought sandwiches, salad, soup and bottles of flavored seltzer at Publix and drove to Samantha's job, Divitiae Pharma. He pulled into the parking lot and texted:

"I'm here."

"Coming out."

Samantha opened the passenger door and kissed Chris.

"Babe, I need you to translate something for me."

"Ok, send them to me."

"I don't want to create any additional trails on these emails before I know what exactly I'm showing to Sclafani. Here, I forwarded emails from a suspect to my old personal email account."

"Fine, let me see." Samantha grabbed his phone. "brosbeersbongsbitches@yahoo.com?"

"I was nineteen. Now I only use it for free trials online."

"Ok. Fine. Which emails?" Samantha said while laughing to herself.

"The ones forwarded from Nissar."

"This one is from Amina Duperville and she's telling Nissar that Alex is going crazy. The next one says Alex was beating her and threatening to kill her and parade her around town for everyone to see. In this one she wants to leave Cap-Haitian and can Nissar send some money? This one is saying mom would have wanted him to help her." Samantha paused.

"I guess they are siblings, I think this woman is Nissar's sister and she's in a bad marriage."

"Oh." Chris was disappointed. It was a waste of time, his sister was getting the shit kicked out of her and asked her brother for help.

"Wait, but this next email is written all in caps and it says: 'Alex is dead.'" Samantha hesitated.

"Oh, shit, she killed him? Will she go to jail for killing her husband in Haiti?"

"It depends on whether she has enough money to pay cops and eyewitnesses, if she does, she won't have to spend any time in jail."

Samantha read through the rest of the emails.

"Well, wait, forget it. It's not what I thought. It's more complicated... I don't understand... Wait, but this and this, look. She sent links."

"Links to what?"

"I'm not sure." Samantha opened a video on Chris's phone. There was an old Haitian lady heaving hysterically.

"A warlock flew through the sky... and, and, and sent them to find Agwe."

"What?"

"And she sent another twenty links describing how he sent... zombies... zombies into the sea."

"This makes no sense."

"I don't get it either." Samantha breathed heavily. "She's saying that someone killed Alex and a group of people in Haiti. I don't know, I don't get it and she wants this guy Nissar to help her. I don't know."

Samantha bit into the roast beef sandwich and was upset. Chris was shocked when Samantha grabbed a napkin to spit out the sandwich before taking several swigs of seltzer.

"What's the matter with you?".

"I can't eat it."

"Why not?"

'The meat isn't cooked, it's still bloody."

"But it's roast beef, if they cooked it all the way, it would be tough and have no flavor."

"Listen, I get it. It's tacky to eat beef well-done. I get it. That's why I always order chicken or fish."

"But why don't you just try it?"

"Listen, Haitian people don't eat bloody meat, never, ever, ever. If you ask my mom, she would say that the animal's soul is still in the blood and you have to cook it all the way through to separate the soul from the body. I don't know if that's true, but, what I do know is that I can't stand the sight of blood, I hate tattoos, needles, scab picking, and I definitely can't eat bloody meat."

"Now I feel bad, because I got you the wrong sandwich."

"I'll have the salad and the rest of the tea that's on my desk."

"I feel horrible, I never noticed that you didn't eat red meat."

"I eat red meat. Burgers, meatloaf, beef stew, it just has to be cooked all the way through. Well-done. Absolutely no pink."

"I feel bad now, like I ruined your day."

"Seeing you for lunch made my day." Samantha said while checking the time on her phone.

"I know, you have to go." Chris kissed her neck.

\*\*\*\*\*

Driving to the station, Chris remembered that Divitiae Pharma held a barbecue before the shooting outbreak. Matt had lamb chops before getting a private lap dance. He never got a chance to eat his own roast beef sandwich and wanted to see how Nissar would react. More than seven hours had passed. Chris found Rodriguez observing Nissar through the two-way mirror.

"You've been here for a while, right Nissar?" Chris asked.

"I'm fine."

"You look Arab to me, man. And your name is Arab, but your green card says you were born in Haiti." Rodriguez said.

"Yes, there are quite a few Arab families in Haiti." Nissar responded in a heavy French accent.

"Oh, so your parents came from where?" Rodriguez asked.

"My parents were born in Haiti."

"How about your grandparents? Rodriguez prodded.

"All four of my grandparents were born in Haiti. I never said I wasn't Haitian."

"What do you do Nissar?" Rodriguez asked.

"I invest in hospitality companies."

"Basically, you're a pimp, you take a cut of the girls' money when they shake asses to make a few dollars."

"The women who work at our establishments are handsomely paid."

"I saw your club. It was an elegant affair."

"Why, thank you."

"Great food, courteous service. You should be proud, you did an excellent job."

"That is nice to hear."

"I am so sorry, forgive us, where are our manners. You've been here all day and we still haven't offered you anything to eat."

Chris unfolded the white wax paper on the roast beef sandwich in front of Nissar.

"Don't worry, it isn't pork."

"I've always eaten pork. I'm not Muslim."

"It's roast beef."

"That'll be fine."

Chris unlocked Nissar's handcuffs. Nissar rubbed his wrists until full sensation returned to his hands. He pushed the wax paper and picked up half of the sandwich. His countenance changed when he peeked inside the sandwich. A deep internal sigh escaped Nissar.

"What's wrong?"

"Oh, nothing. I'm fine."

"Let me guess, the roast beef is still bloody."

"I can't eat it. I don't eat meat that hasn't been fully cooked."

"Really, why is that?"

"I don't know. We don't eat raw meat. Listen, you could place this sandwich on the street in Haiti and even the poorest person wouldn't eat it."

"Yeah, I get that, but why?"

"It's the way it is."

"So you won't eat raw meat?"

"No."

"But you serve it to the customers at your clubs?"

"We are there to please the customers, in every way, shape and form."

"I know you did this."

"Did what?"

"You drugged those girls."

"Those girls used drugs."

"No, you put something in their drugs."

"Listen, I am not a drug dealer. Drugs deal themselves. I do not make or sell drugs. Drugs are filled with noxious additives. Those girls should have been more careful. The same people who are quick to criticize the lack of governmental food regulations, pay three times as much for organic apples, attend anti-GMO protests but then turn right around and snort coke. Cocaine is, and has always been, cut with shit, from talcum powder, rat poison, diarrhea medicine, other drugs and God knows whatever else. Those girls got bad batches of drugs and it made them go crazy. No jury in the state of Florida is going to blame me for strippers who died snorting coke. Never gonna happen."

"And the dead bodies of the male customers?"

"Again, people crazy out of their minds on cocaine. I have no idea what happens to men when they leave the strip club. That's their business."

"You don't mind talking to us without an attorney?"

"Absolutely not. Nothing you throw at me will ever stick. I'll tell you exactly what will happen: first the prosecutor will lose different pieces of my case file, next the court calendar will be disorganized, then you'll see a series of judges being reassigned and chaos will come in every form until the case disappears. Confusion will be sown until nothing can be moved forward.

"You sound confident." Rodriguez said.

"I'm not confident. I'm patient."

"What are you waiting patiently for?"

"If you only knew."

"Listen, we know you were in contact with Spencer Warren. These shredded bodies were found around your strip club and at his pharmaceutical company." Chris said composed.

"Ha."

"You think I'm funny. Who is Alex Duperville?" Chris asked.

A flash of anger rose inside of Nissar. His veil was pierced by carelessness.

Nissar put on his best poker face in an effort to not reveal any more information than necessary.

"Well, I meant to say 'who was Alex Duperville?'"

"What do you know about Haiti?"

"I thought you weren't afraid of the American legal system and had plenty of money to hire lawyers?"

"Lawyers? Who would be stupid enough to put their life in the hands of a lawyer? All I have to do is call my *bòkò* to cast spells --- attorneys, cops, judges, and anyone related to the case would bend and the case eventually thrown out."

"You forgot to erase your sister's emails telling you her husband Alex was dead."

"You know what, you are knocking on doors that you don't want answered. You think you're in charge. You think you have power. You have no idea what has been unleashed or the things that are coming. Your limited ability to comprehend the world is about to be fucked. I'll be fine. People like me; we go from country to country and leave when calamity strikes. Where are you going? The spells that have been cast go beyond simple confusion, chaos and delays. It is worse than dead bodies in Miami, bigger than dead bodies in Haiti. A shift in spiritual power has been opened and no one knows what is going to happen.

My family is originally from Syria. We practiced our own magic before we ever arrived in Haiti. My great grandfather was recognized for his mastery of the spirits. Forced out of Syria, they chose Haiti because of its unbridled spiritual power. He was admitted into the highest realms of Haitian mysteries. You know nothing about Haiti. The door between our world and the spirit worlds are located in Haiti. What you don't know can hurt you. By the looks on your faces, I can tell you don't believe a word I've said."

Chris was normally content to play the back bench and avoid confrontation but Nissar unsettled him. It was worse than the attack on his best friend and heavier than the savagery of bloody bodies strewn across Miami Beach; disdain framed every word that came out of Nissar. A silent anger turned his face beet red as he clenched his fists white. Nissar's permanent sneer grated on Chris's nerves. He was ready to punch Nissar when an emergency alarm rang. Rodriguez and Chris gazed at the loudspeaker in disbelief.

"This is not a drill. I repeat, this is not a drill. Please report to your assigned emergency protocol meeting point. This is not a drill."

Through the precinct window, people were running across the beach away from the restaurants lining Ocean Drive. Colleagues nervously donned riot gear stored in a dusty storage room. There was no time for paperwork, no time to scan and assign each piece to a different cop as procedure would normally require. One after one, Chris, Rodriguez and the other cops appeared in full length Plexiglas shields, military grade riot helmets, arm braces and a seemingly never-ending supply of semi-automatic weapons. Captain Sclafani was the last to appear. He mustered his deepest voice:

"Just off an emergency conference call with the police departments in North Miami, South Miami, Northside, Miami Shores, Dade-County PD--- we have a crisis on our hands. There have been reports of people biting people's faces and necks everywhere. It's full blown mayhem. I don't know what this is, and guess what--- it doesn't matter, we have to go out there. There is no other way."

Sclafani fuddled with the helmet in his hands and moved towards the main precinct entrance. People were racing through the streets. Chris hoped Samantha was safe. He tried calling her and got busy signals.

People ran to the precinct from all directions. A blonde woman lost a shoe while running, two teenage boys hurdled over a bus stop bench and an older man tripped on his own feet on the entranceway approaching the precinct. Younger cops in SWAT gear were sent outside first as men and women dashed for cover. On the beach, their nightmares had come true. Carnivorous people were devouring others in broad daylight. Bedlam struck hard.

Bodies with superhuman strength were knocking people down to feed on their flesh. One woman's breast was bitten off through her bikini while others dropped to feed on the rest of her body. The first batch of SWAT officers retreated from the water. Another dozen cops climbed on top of a mail truck with their state-issued Ruger 10/22's to shoot everything that moved. It was impossible to distinguish between the fearful and those feeding on freshly torn flesh. Sclafani watched the carnage before sending another dozen officers into the fray.

"Take the cars. Drive up and down the beach. It'll be easier to shoot out of the windows than to run through the chaos." Sclafani yelled as they bolted through the doors.

Chris called Samantha and couldn't get through. He tried to call his parents; the line was busy. Nothing was working. While he tried other numbers on his phone, helicopters appeared above. He joined Sclafani and the other cops outside of the protection of the precinct's reinforced doors. They assumed military reinforcements were coming to save them and despaired when the private helicopter flew south without stopping to provide assistance.

A drove of zombies came down the nearest street. Chris and Rodriguez communicated without using words. Rodriguez tilted his head, he was about to bail. His wife and three kids were his priority in the midst of this shit storm. Sclafani and a group of cops stepped past the war memorial in front of the police station. Rodriguez inconspicuously abandoned his colleagues and drove home.

An errant mass of flesh seeking bodies hurdled towards the precinct. The cops tried to run back into the station house. Hundreds of unconscious hungry bodies scurried through sidewalk cafes, hotel lobbies and side streets off Ocean Drive. The scent of raw flesh galvanized the herd. Pop, pop, pop, pop, pop,

pop, pop, pop. Shots rang in all directions from the cops holding their positioned on top of the mail truck. A zombie climbed the truck and knocked an officer down while tearing a long piece of flesh from the side of his face before biting violently into the jugular vein. There was animalistic disconnect in each zombie bite.

The soulless cannibalistic crowd surrounded the precinct. The cornered cops created a cacophony of rapid fire. Pop, whip, tsk, whew, plop... pop, pop, pop, pop, pop, pop, pop, pop. Bullets went forth until a guttural scream threw Sclafani to the ground. In the midst of the calamity he forgot to put on his helmet. A bullet intended for the zombies had scattered chunks of Sclafani's brain all over the sidewalk leading to the police precinct. Chris's knees nearly buckled in disbelief. He barely caught his breath when more deranged bodies approached him. Sclafani's dead body killed any remaining courage within the precinct. Cops abandoned their positions and scurried in different directions.

Chris had one thought on his mind: Samantha.

# TALC

# 17 SAMANTHA SAVIN

*Miami Beach, Florida*

Samantha had questions about the mysterious powder found on the dead bodies. Her direct supervisor was dead. She needed permission from human resources to run tests on the mysterious powder in another on-site laboratory. Instead of making a lab available, Samantha received explicit instructions from human resources to compile a comprehensive report on her decimated department. Sally, the vice president of human resources, was nice but didn't understand lab work. Whenever Samantha followed-up with a clarifying question, she was told questions would be answered at the business continuity meeting on Wednesday.

It was Wednesday afternoon and no one had any additional information. As the newest and only remaining member of the gene therapy team, Samantha was supposed to summarize their work before the business continuity committee. She received the meeting confirmation less than seventy-two hours ago, sixteen other departments would also be in attendance. The entire gene therapy team was slaughtered and she was supposed to give a presentation. Samantha reviewed her report. She sorted her team's shared files from the last two weeks and drafted her report on the temporarily installed computers in the east wing of Divitiae Pharma. Samantha printed out the presentation and corrected it with a red pen to make sure it was as accurate as it could be; she rearranged graphs and charts on the slides. Forty minutes before the meeting, she rushed to proofread the report on the initiatives and results catalogued by the genetic therapy team before the outbreak.

Samantha balanced a leather padfolio, iPad, telephone, and individually wrapped butter mints in her arms and dragged herself into the executive conference room. Samantha tried to quiet the nerves rising within her. She reminded herself to say as little as possible. Less is more. Provide a brief status update on the work that had been coordinated by the team before they died. With increased access to the shared drives by IT, she sorted the documents by last saved, edited and opened and compiled them into a report sorted by each person and project. Samantha highlighted project corrections, inserted lab results and data, noted written article sources, calculated numeric formulas applied, summarized chemical purchase orders, and explained experiment results. She included as much scientific information as possible and omitted her suspicions.

Samantha knew better than to include her feelings or intuitions. When around white people, at work, and especially around scientists, Samantha only discussed data and information with verifiable sources. Right now, there was nothing she could prove. All she could do was provide an account of final projects and work summaries of her dead colleagues.

She recognized some of the faces in the conference room. The heads of various departments, security, accounting, human resources, IT, procurement, and even Spencer Warren, the chairman's chief-of-staff, were present. People droned on trying to impress each other while Samantha jotted questions to research later, added items to her to-do list and stored mental notes on the attendees who gave her the creeps.

One by one, each department provided an accounting of their strategic response and plan to meet quarterly and yearly objectives. No one mentioned, let alone asked the question that was on everyone's mind. What the fuck happened? Why did their colleagues start eating people? It had been more than three days since the gruesome carnage took place in Divitiae Pharma and everyone was working sixteen hour days. Yet no one had the courage to speak frankly about the horrific death of their co-workers. Everyone spoke in euphemisms-- since the tragedy, untimely loss, unfortunate circumstances. They used phrases to avoid the truth: their co-workers started eating each other at work and were shot down. Was no one going to discuss that people got killed?

The conference room was full of bean counters. Samantha, at twenty-nine, was the youngest person in the room and was dismayed at their mind-numbing expressions and callousness. The insensitivity of these people was astounding. There was no light or love to be found in them. They no longer thought for themselves. Every uttered sentence was rehearsed to win friends and influence people around a water cooler. They moved forward, step by step, with glassy eyes and didn't have the wherewithal to think for themselves. They mindlessly repeated the exact same phrases, like "stealing your thunder" we need to "loop them into the conversation" "the value-add" "corporate priorities" and other ridiculous refrains. No one was thinking critically, no one was asking the important questions. They rehashed what they were expected to report.

Department heads deferentially addressed their nonsensical corporate ramblings in an apparent attempt to please Spencer Warren, which was impossible. Spencer Warren didn't smile or smirk. He didn't complain or compliment. He listened and memorized everything with a casual uncommitted ease.

Spencer's face gave away nothing until Jared Smith, vice president for facilities, explained how an exterminator was called on Monday, the day after the unfortunate incident. Puddles of stagnant water had accumulated beneath the large broken glass tanks containing mosquitos and ticks. The Divitiae Pharma site was unbearable when the cleaning staff arrived on Monday morning. Visible swarms of mosquitoes and ticks inhabited the north end of the compound. The police were still conducting their investigation and the exterminator was not allowed to fumigate. As a result, an increased number of mosquitos inhabited the building.

"Thanks, Jared, you said that the research insects were released?" Spencer Warren said with a raised eyebrow.

"Yes, and we are working day and night with the exterminators to get the situation under control."

"I understand, thank you everyone. We will reconvene in forty-eight hours and provide detailed information to the rest of our partners."

Before anyone could get out of their seats, rumbling screeches cut through the false serenity forged by the business continuity committee. Samantha tried to identify the source of the screams and massive stampede sounds that approached them. And through the glass doors, Divitiae Pharma employees ran and screamed down the hallways. Her older white colleagues remained motionless and asked each other questions as a surge of employees ran past them.

Samantha sprung out of her chair. She didn't ask any questions; she raced out of the conference room. Shredded blood soaked bodies were in the distant end of the hallway. She hurdled over the front desk and didn't stop running. Once outside, Samantha jumped into her makeshift office, secured her purse and grabbed the car keys off the desk, kicked off her high heels and discovered a reserve of speed that got her to the parking lot.

There was no denying the truth. The cause of their fear was zombies. Infected Divitiae Pharma employees were searching for fresh flesh. Some cried, others screamed. People scattered in all directions as she climbed into her unlocked car. Samantha gathered her thoughts. The car was in reverse and she slammed the accelerator with her bare foot and knocked down three infected employees. Another woman with a blood covered mouth tried to open the driver side door. Samantha drove and left everything behind her. Samantha was afraid and didn't know what to do. Her instinct told her to go home, and wherever Chris was, was home.

# 18 THE CHAIRMAN

*Miami Beach, Florida*

Spencer Warren immediately focused his efforts on ensuring the Chairman's safety. He ran in the opposite direction of his petrified colleagues, past the security access doors and directly into the Chairman's suite. It was an expansive space which encompassed the entire fourth floor which led to a rooftop terrace large enough to host the massive company Christmas party. Spencer Warren found the Chairman, as frail as he was, not seated in his hover chair but standing by the terrace railing surveying his life's work. An unidentified noise grew. The Chairman turned and Spencer Warren scurried in like a lapdog.

"Sir, I really must insist that we get you to safety. It appears that we have another outbreak on the property and this time the building is full of personnel. We must take steps to ensure that you do not remain in harm's way." Spencer insisted.

"Thank you for your concern. I already called Allen and asked him to bring the helicopter."

Spencer took a deep breath of relief, rubbed his forehead and his sense of worry seemed to dissipate.

"We will need to destroy certain records and take steps to mitigate harm. Aside from that, I already compiled a team to start working through the damage control strategy. We need to put together strategic messaging for the media, public and governmental officials, we have the situation well under control."

The Chairman stared at Spencer with a mix of disdain and contempt; he was expendable. People like Spencer were constantly searching for a leader, someone to follow, someone to validate them. The Chairman found them utterly disgusting; no matter how useful they were to him in the short term. Men like Spencer who allowed other men to prescribe the course of their lives deserved to be towed to the scrap heap. Men who lived for the sake of other men were disposable. They lacked vision and were nonessential. At a young age they aspired to please their parents, teachers, and coaches, which culminated in an insatiable desire to please their bosses. And it was the root of their insignificance.

Life isn't about mitigation-- the spoils go to the bold. The men who dare to take a chance and push the boundaries. America has grown fearful. He would not let his irreplaceable fire be extinguished in the hopeless quicksand of no. America used to take the big steps. Now it waits on the sidelines while the Chinese use CRISPR on human embryos and the Cas9 protein scissor through genes. If anyone is going to slice through DNA and unlock the potential to make a better human gene pool... it was going to be Divitiae Pharma. Germline editing is the future. Sitting by and doing nothing while prissy academics complain was not an option.

The Chairman left grad school with nothing but twenty five dollars in his back pocket and a capacity to think. His own father was a failure, and was sure he would fail too. Starting a business was inherently risky, but that did not dissuade the Chairman. As a child, he was convinced he would rather sell hot dogs from his own cart than cater to the caprices of other men.

The last person the Chairman ever loved was his wife and she died nearly thirty years ago. His son was a degenerate gambler who invented unimaginative ways to waddle through his trust fund, a dim-witted embarrassment. What motivated the Chairman was a desire to learn, to advance and to do more. His brand new heart should give him at least another ten years.

His first order of business was to leverage this outbreak to consolidate power. To find the solution, he needed to return where it all began: Haiti.

As a young chemical engineer on a day cruise between Cuba and Haiti in the 1950's, the Chairman had met Mathieu, a tour guide who specialized in taking people off the beaten tourist paths to the Citadelle. He paid Mathieu a handsome sum to introduce him to the *houngans* and *bòkò* throughout the north of Haiti. He gave the men, most of them illiterate and living in hidden corners of the countryside, crisp twenty dollar bills for the recipes of their natural treatments. Many of the Chairman's earliest pharmaceutical successes were based on peasant formulas purchased for less than two hundred dollars.

The Chairman refined the rudimentary recipes in his garage laboratory until he isolated the healing components. He didn't believe in the superstitions of Haiti. Vodou was an anthropological repository of generations of human knowledge and complex morality plays responding to challenges endured by locals. While others were afraid, he ruthlessly mined obscure Vodou spells for practical applications. Once he had the basic recipes, he hired staff to tweak the accuracy, potency and delivery methods. Slowly he earned enough money to hire detailed marketing and public relations firms to establish Divitiae Pharma's reputation. Those formulas became the foundation of his multibillion dollar pharmaceutical empire.

The Chairman wasn't worried about the carnage he witnessed from the terraced rooftop. The earth's population was growing out of control and it was only a matter of time until nature took matters into her own hands to address the overpopulation issue. His longtime use of zombie powder on his own Divitiae Pharma employees rendered them docile, unassertive and accommodating to every corporate request. The Chairman was surprised that the increased dosage of zombie powder in the company ventilation system had caused such an immediate adverse effect. He didn't realize it would come so soon, or that he would be alive to witness the natural clearing of the inferiors.

The Chairman turned and Spencer Warren's incessant chatter was unbearable. It was time to end these useless conversations. Spencer was the only person who knew that the Chairman brought zombies and zombie powder formula to Miami. Spencer had full knowledge of the Chairman's elaborate scheme to bring himself back from the dead and cheat death. The zombie talc powder formula contained the essential components to interrupt death and with new gene therapy technology Divitiae Pharma was set to master the mystery separating life from death.

While Spencer rambled, the Chairman hypothesized that a cross-contamination between the zombie powder and the gene therapy caused this minor inconvenience. His original goal was to reprogram the gene sequences of the Zombie Deer Disease, the Lone Star Tick which caused meat allergies, and the Zika carrying mosquitos to identify, isolate and edit the genes that control blood and muscle regeneration. The experimentation pool started with the insects and progressed to strippers and other undesirables around Miami. It was time for the Chairman to assemble a new team. None of them could be made privy to the true origins of Divitiae Pharma's role in harnessing Haitian zombie powder.

The Chairman used Spencer to find prostitutes and strippers across Miami to test the different formulas. They were already drugged out of their minds, and once involved in sex work or addicted to crack, meth or heroin--- no medical examiner's office would conduct more than a perfunctory assessment on the cause of death. Any bodily damage they incurred would not be thoroughly investigated.

It was Divitiae Pharma's secret to gaining FDA approvals over the last fifty years. In the 1960's, they tested medicine in rural Haiti, but the Chairman hated the additional expense of shipping medical equipment and employee travel. The constant bribes to the Duvalier regime were not enough to guarantee continuous electricity for petri dishes, centrifuges and sample refrigeration. Even more burdensome, the seventies brought a new wave of medical ethics and American medical researchers grew hesitant to perform what they called unethical tests in Haiti. It killed company morale. The type of recruits who were willing to conduct unethical human subject tests normally graduated at the bottom of their class and were the worst types. The Chairman simply could not tolerate mediocrity in his company and had an ironclad rule of only hiring the best and the brightest.

The 1970's cocaine epidemic solved his problem. Plenty of women willingly signed releases and underwent experimental drug treatments in return for hundreds of dollars. The researchers no longer had to manage the guilt of taking advantage of illiterate islanders. The new test subjects were attractive and appeared healthy; there was no ethical burden to bear. Participants were paid handsome sums to ingest an entire spectrum of trial drugs. Attractive young women were also willing to conveniently suck dicks during research appointments and allowed Divitiae Pharma scientists to make it home in time for dinner with their wives and kids.

Spencer was the last person with knowledge of the different moving pieces. This outbreak was more than even the Chairman could have imagined. He went into his desk for a quick release needle and leered at Spencer, who never seemed to take a breath. The Chairman smiled.

"I wanted to thank you for your help, Spencer. This company couldn't have grown without you over the last dozen years."

Spencer was shocked; he had never received a compliment or a positive acknowledgment of his work in his time as chief-of-staff. He fought the warm sensation of tears.

The Chairman shook his hand while his left hand quickly stuck a tiny syringe filled with a deadly mixture into Spencer's ribs. Spencer flinched and had no idea that the short muscle spasm on his side meant his death. It would kill Spencer in two days and the Chairman would be far away. Both men felt the powerful winds of the helicopter landing on the rooftop.

"Where are you going, sir?"

"I'm going to think about a few things."

"I will have my cell phone on me at all times."

"That's good to know." The Chairman said as he smiled at him one last time.

The Chairman walked steadily despite his frailty and ducked to board the helicopter. Spencer gave the Chairman a helping hand into the passenger seat and closed the door. The pilot pointed his thumb up and Spencer backed away as the helicopter soared.

"Where to, sir?" The pilot inquired.

"Head south, we're going to Haiti."

# ACKNOWLEDGEMENTS

I am forever grateful for Robert Benfatto's patient and loving insight. My deepest thanks to Dahoud André for his powerful advocacy on behalf of Kreyòl and Vodou culture in this work of fiction. Genuine appreciation to Solape Lawal-Solarin for his enthusiasm in helping this book put its best foot forward. Gratitude to Wale Emosu for his detailed feedback.

# ABOUT THE AUTHOR

Jenna Chrisphonte is the author of *Talc: A Haitian Zombie Story.* Chrisphonte was born in Haiti and reared in New York. She is currently writing a dramatic trilogy-- Property: *The Rule in Shelly's Case, Rule Against Perpetuities* and *Adverse Possession.* Her dramatic work has been presented at the Classical Theatre of Harlem, Dixon Place and WOW Café Theater. Chrisphonte's professional experience includes work for the Dramatists Guild of America, the Lillys, Global Affairs Canada, the French Ministry of National Education, the State University of New York and Manhattan Community Board 4. She holds Bachelor's and Juris Doctor degrees from the University at Buffalo. Chrisphonte divides her time between New York and Brussels.

chrisphonte.com

Jenna Chrisphonte
@talcahaitianzombiestory
@jchrisphonte79
@jennachrisphonte

Made in the USA
Las Vegas, NV
07 May 2022

48545326R10157